Below the Far Horizon

RASPBERRY RIDGE
BOOK EIGHT

JESSIE GUSSMAN

Contents

Acknowledgments

Cover art by Julia Gussman
Editing by Heather Hayden
Narration by Jay Dyess
Author Services by CE Author Assistant

Listen to the unabridged audio for FREE performed by Jay Dyess on the Say with Jay channel on YouTube. Get early access to all of Jay's recordings and listen to Jessie's books before they're available to the general public, plus get daily Bible readings by Jay and bonus scenes by becoming a Say with Jay channel member.

One

Grace Tyack pulled into the driveway at her mother's house in Raspberry Ridge, the town in which she grew up, and pulled in a deep breath of cool, fresh lake air.

Everything still looked the same. Large trees shaded the street that dead-ended at the edge of a cliff, the base of which was surrounded by Pebble Beach, that rocky stretch of shore that lead to Lake Michigan.

The healing garden that was now at the end of the road, before the cliff, hadn't been there when she'd been growing up, but that was one of the few changes.

A couple big houses on the hill she remembered from childhood looked lived in and cheerful rather than old and imposing the way she remembered them, but it could be her different perspective as an adult rather than any specific changes that had been made.

Her mother's house was a block back from the dead end. Grace had been dreading the end of her trip, so she'd driven to the healing garden, sat there for a bit, and turned around.

She'd been tempted to park and walk through it, but she didn't want to meet anyone she knew.

She was saving all of her courage to face her mother.

It seemed the time had come.

Her sisters, Stacy and Jill, would be there too. They had been taking care of their mother during her hip replacement from the beginning at the hospital with her and had gone through the first week of dealing with the aftermath of surgery and the hardest part of the pain.

They both needed to go back to their jobs, and Grace... Grace didn't have a job to go back to.

Taking another deep, cleansing breath, dreading the conversation she was going to have to have with all of her heart, Grace forced herself to touch the handle of the door before she yanked it and stepped out.

It was a BMW, and she owed too much on it to sell it and get out from underneath it. So she kept it, although she had no idea how she was going to make the payments. She'd missed last month, and late notices were piling up in her mailbox.

That was one of the reasons she did not leave a forwarding address.

That, and while she knew her mother would be fine with her moving in permanently, her mother did not yet know that her husband had cheated on her and left, that the papers for her divorce were signed.

Her mother also didn't know that she was currently unemployed.

Yeah. Some success story she was. Her mother was sure to be proud.

Gritting her teeth and flexing her lips, practicing a smile that felt more like a snarl, she lifted her head and put her shoulders back. She wasn't going to go slinking into the house. She had her pride after all. And she'd left town full of sass and confidence, sure that she was going to take the world by storm, beat it into submission, and come out on top.

That wasn't exactly what had happened.

Tulips bloomed along the wall, the same tulips that had come up every year of Grace's life. Red and purple and yellow and pink. Pretty and regal, the day they poked through the ground was always the day she finally felt she had evidence for the promise of spring.

Winters along the shores of Lake Michigan could be cold and brutal. To put it mildly. Grace thought anyone and anything who could grow up enduring those kinds of conditions would have to be strong and hardy.

But she hadn't exactly been strong and hardy as she fumbled and mumbled her way into the city, married the wrong man, got a job that she hated, and basically made a mess of her life.

Just the fact that you survived all of that means you are strong and hardy.

The voice spoke in her head as she put one foot on the porch step.

Really? Was it just the idea that she hadn't been brought to her knees, begging God for mercy, that meant that she was stronger than she thought she was?

Or maybe it was the idea that it wasn't her strength but the Lord's. Because that was the one thing that the events of the last year had taught her. The religion of her childhood had a place in her life.

She continued on the steps and then paused at the door. Should she knock?

She'd been back a couple of times for Christmas, staying only as long as necessary.

Her husband had come with her once, but the second time she'd come, he'd insisted that he needed to stay and work and couldn't take the time away from his job to accompany her to her home for Christmas.

She hadn't given him a hard time, because he hadn't been back to see his parents the entire time they'd been together. She'd never met them. She didn't even know if they really existed or if he'd hatched or maybe been dropped out of an alien spacecraft, considering all the lies he told her over the years. Lies that hadn't come out until she figured out that he had been cheating on her, regularly, behind her back. His late nights of working had actually been meeting other women at bars. His work-related expenses had been hotel bills, sure, but they were for the women that he'd hooked up with behind her back.

And she had been blissfully unaware.

What a farce her marriage had been. The one saving grace was the fact that her husband had adamantly refused her request to consider having children. She had begged and pleaded, wanting to start a family, buoyed by memories of her own family growing up beside the shores of Lake Michigan. They had been happy, idyllic days. Days she wanted to recapture, and maybe she thought the best way to do that would be to have a family of her own.

Still, her husband had adamantly refused. And Grace had ended up being happy about that, after all of the details of his exploits had come out.

Maybe not all of them. She actually didn't know if she knew all of them or not. Maybe there were things he had done behind her back that she had never found out about. That was quite possible. He wasn't exactly known as an honest person or someone who ever told the truth. Ever.

She almost snorted. Her ex was the kind of person who didn't tell the truth if a lie would suffice.

The clean lake breeze lifted her hair. That part of her life was over now. She tried to push it out of her mind and focus on the conversation she would be having when she stepped in the door.

Deciding a combination of knocking and walking in would be the best move, she rapped on the door before she opened it and stepped inside.

She had prepared herself for seeing her mother and the questions that her family would invariably ask. The confrontation of her sisters over the fact that she was broke, jobless, husbandless, and driving a BMW that may or may not be repossessed in the near future. All of those things she expected, and felt she deserved, to be grilled on.

What she hadn't expected was the way the scent of her mother's home, familiar and beloved and bringing back all of the happy and wishful memories of her youth, would hit her.

She was still reeling from the slightly yeasty smell, mixed with flowers and her mother's hand cream, when Stacy, her older sister, appeared in the doorway of the living room.

"I thought you were coming yesterday," Stacy said, in lieu of a greeting apparently.

Grace reminded herself that she needed to be humble. She'd been proud for way too long.

"I'm sorry. I...got held up." Not by anything in particular. Just by her own cowardice. She didn't want to leave her home, the home she lived in since she got married ten years prior. Her husband had claimed it had been a gift from his parents. Now she wondered. But what else would it have been? His paramours hadn't exactly been giving him money. It was the other way around.

Even though it had been a year since she first found out, pain still balled up inside of her. Maybe she was paying for all the lost dreams or for the way that she had been determined to make a success of herself. To show everyone that even though she was a small-town girl, she could play on the big stage.

And maybe it had to do with the fact that she was running from the memories, the tragedy that she never thought about and that she wanted to overcome. To have so much success in her life that she never had to look back and think about what might have been. What she lost, what the people of this town lost.

"Mom is in the den. She prefers that room to this one, as you would know if you had been here at all."

"That's the way it was when we were little. I guess I remember."

Stacy gave her an eye. Maybe at the humility in her tone. Then she lifted her head in acknowledgment, turned around, and started marching toward the den. Grace looked toward the kitchen, the bright cheerfulness still familiar and beckoning her, but she ignored the call. She needed to go see her mom. And Jill, her younger sister. Get those introductions and interrogations out of the way. If all three of them were in the room with her, perhaps she would only have to do this once.

Her mom sat on the couch, a soft blanket over her, wearing a comfy brown top, not jammies, although a worn pair of slippers sat beside the couch. They were not the slippers her mom had worn when she had been a child. Had those worn out? Been lost? Grace hadn't been around enough to know.

"Grace!" her mother said, looking up and holding her arms out.

Gita Honea was a naturally optimistic, happy person who'd made Grace's childhood idyllic. She'd been the perfect mother, as far as Grace could tell, even though Grace had gone through a period of rebellion in her teenage years, like every teenager did, right?

That wasn't true. She'd known teens who had grown closer to their parents during those years. Unfortunately, she didn't have that kind of wisdom at the time to know that was the best way for a person's life to go.

Now she did, but now was way too late. She wanted to apologize to her mother for the grief she caused during those years. But this wasn't the time.

"Did you find out why she wasn't here yesterday?" Jill asked as she walked into the den behind them.

Stacy shook her head.

"I want a hug first," Gita said, continuing to hold out her arms.

Grace walked forward, embracing her mother, reveling in the familiar scent of vanilla and yeast and something sweet and dear to her heart.

It was the scent in this house that had turned her heart and stomach inside out.

That's what was going to make this next conversation more difficult, because the scent had brought back all of the love and laughter, and the tragedy too.

She straightened, her mother making sure to continue to grip her hands.

"I'm so glad you're here. I've missed you so much. I've only seen you a couple of times in the last decade."

That was a little bit of an underrepresentation of the truth. Grace had been here at least three times in the last ten years. And her mother had visited a handful of times in Indianapolis, where they'd settled.

Still, it hadn't been nearly enough. And Grace could honestly say, "I'm glad to be home."

She didn't think now was the time to tell her mother that she was broke, didn't have a job, and was hoping to move in with her. That would come later, after her sisters had left.

"I'm only able to stay until tomorrow. So you're going to have to learn everything that you need to do pretty quickly," Stacy said. Always the one in charge. She was the perfect daughter. She lived just down the beach in Strawberry Sands, and she had the perfect family, a son and a daughter, a husband whose employer was in Chicago, although he worked from home three days a week.

Her life couldn't be any more perfect. She intimidated Grace, and perhaps Grace had spent so much time trying to be perfect, just so she could keep up with her sister.

"I have to leave tomorrow too. So it's going to be all on you after that, Grace." Jill echoed her older sister's words.

Jill also had a perfect life, although she and her husband were childless. Still, they lived close, although further west and not right along the lake. But she was a nurse at a local hospital, and her husband was a doctor.

"You girls worry too much. Grace is perfectly capable of taking care of me, and she's completely cleared her calendar for the next six weeks, which is so generous and sweet of her." Her mother looked at her with so much admiration and love Grace could hardly stand it.

"You're worth it, Mom," she said and tried to put some genuine feeling behind it, because she did believe it. But she felt so guilty because the words her mom said weren't even close to being true. She had nowhere else to go. That's why she was here. Although, she would certainly help take care of her mom as she recovered. It would have just been a little bit more difficult to juggle her schedule.

"I'm going to show you a few things, and then Jill and I are going to go out for lunch. We've been here twenty-four/seven since we got here, and we deserve a little time off." Stacy spoke like it was a given, although somehow her words made Grace feel like she was being left out. Of course, she could have come two weeks ago, but the idea of being with her mom in the hospital, under all that pressure, and scared to death as to whether or not she would make it, and then all of the pain and suffering after she got out. She just couldn't stand the idea. And then the papers had arrived, needing her signature.

That threw her for another loop and kept her away another week. The idea of confronting her sisters and admitting what her life was like was the reason she had delayed one more day.

She didn't want to delay anymore.

That wasn't true. She wanted to, but she wasn't going to allow herself to. Digging deep, she took a breath and then met her older and most intimidating sister right in the eye. "Stacy, if you wouldn't mind, I have something I need to tell all of you, and since we're all here, this is a good time."

Stacy blinked, like she couldn't believe that there was something in her sister's life that she didn't know about. Still, her sister's usually busy hands were quiet in front of her, and she waited, as though this were going to be a one-sentence explanation and then she could get on with her life.

"I think you probably should sit down." Grace realized her voice sounded very timid. She tried to infuse confidence in it. "And, Mom, I'm sorry to do this to you when you're not feeling the best—"

Her mom waved a hand. "I feel fine. A little bit of pain occasionally, but the girls have been great at keeping up with the pill schedule, and I've been able to do all of my physical therapy, and I'm well ahead of the norm, which is what my therapist said."

She probably should ask after her mother's health and how the surgery went and all that. They'd been in touch via text and phone calls, but not nearly as much as her mother would have preferred.

"That's good. It sounds like you're going to be up and about in no time."

"I hope so. My craft supply is getting rather low. The girls have been great at mailing the things out, but you are the only one who was ever able to make anything even remotely similar to what I can."

Grace nodded, knowing what her mom said was true. She was the only one that had inherited their mom's artistic flair. The other two girls were way too serious and analytical to be able to do anything even remotely artistic. Still, they could package up the crafts as they were ordered online and ship them out, as their mom had just said. That didn't take any kind of artistic flair at all, except perhaps wrapping them.

"I'm feeling so well that I probably could start making things again, and I've had so much time to just sit and scroll through different social media and websites that my ideas are practically overflowing in my brain."

For the first time since she'd come, Grace felt a little trickle of excitement. She could help her mom out. She would be good at that. But is that really what she wanted out of her life? To sit at home and make crafts and sell them online? Where was the prestige in that? She had wanted more out of her life, and people had expected more out of her.

She didn't want to let them down, but that was ironic, considering that she already had.

"Well?" Jill asked, perched on the edge of the imitation leather recliner that sat next to the couch.

Two

Stacy had gracefully folded herself into a chair right beside her mother's feet, with a hand, gentle and comforting, on Gita's ankle.

"Well, I figured you guys were going to hear this eventually, probably sooner than later considering how small towns are." She hadn't had to worry about how small towns were for a really long time. That had been one of her considerations whenever she had decided to come. Her whole family was going to know exactly what happened.

She tried not to think about anything other than her story, not the nervousness that spun like sticky spiderwebs in her stomach, or the disappointment that was sure to be on her mother's face, and perhaps the gloating and I-told-you-so look that her sisters would have.

"I was fired from my job two months ago."

"No! I mean, you didn't really like that job, but you made good money," Stacy said immediately. And she looked truly distressed.

She was absolutely right on too. Which surprised Grace. Like Stacy had actually paid attention to her over the years, the few times they talked. Her job overseeing the various departments of the private university where she worked had not been a job that she loved, but it had paid really well.

"At least your husband still has work," Jill said, and Grace assumed that was her way of trying to comfort her.

"Yes." Her fingers picked at the hem of her shirt. "Only he had multiple affairs, and I signed the divorce papers before I left Indianapolis. They're in the back of my car."

"You divorced?" her mother said, the comfort and concern in her tone almost making tears come to Grace's eyes.

"Yes. We're officially divorced. The judge just needs to file the papers. I need to mail them to my lawyer. I didn't take the time to do that." She was supposed to have done it yesterday, which was ostensibly the reason that she stayed home, but she hadn't gotten out of bed except to go to the bathroom. Her shades were drawn, and she'd spent the day crying. Thank goodness for eye drops, since it had taken an entire bottle to make her eyes presentable today.

"Oh my goodness. I didn't know there was any trouble at all," her mother said, pushing up with her elbows before Stacy reached over and motioned for her to stay down. At first, Grace didn't think that Gita was going to listen, but she relaxed back into the couch after wincing.

"Yeah. I didn't want to bother anyone. It was...difficult." To say the least. She had built a life based on the two of them being together forever. She certainly hadn't expected anything to happen to him and certainly had never even dreamed that he might cheat.

"So yeah, I'm jobless, divorced, and I'm behind on most of my bills. He hasn't been paying me, and up until I lost my job, there was no leg for me to stand on because I made as much as he did. I hardly think a judge is going to reverse that just because I got fired. Especially considering that happened almost a year after we separated."

Thankfully he had moved out, although it had taken her dipping into her savings to be able to make the mortgage on their condo by herself. They had definitely overextended on that. Not that she'd had much say in it, since her husband had originally said it was a gift from his parents. It was a gift she'd ended up paying for. And then there was her car payment. She paid it, because she knew she was going to take it with her, but after she lost her job, the severance package was just enough for her to pay her share of the lawyer fees for the divorce and the closing cost for the house. She had literally nothing.

"I'm so sorry to hear that. I thought you were doing fine." Jill stood up and walked over, putting a hand on Grace's shoulder almost as though to check the temperature before she leaned down and gave her a warm hug.

Grace hadn't been sure what to expect from her sisters. They hadn't been especially close growing up. Although, she liked them both, and they talked some. Still, they'd drifted even further apart after they'd all gotten their own families, and Grace had made no effort to stay close.

She'd been busy trying to make her life a success, and she supposed also to make herself relevant compared to them.

The room was quiet for a bit, the silence feeling heavy and hard, before Stacy said, "What are you going to do?"

The question she dreaded. The unknown was always scary. "Well, right now I'm going to take care of Mom. That's what I'm going to do for the next six weeks."

"And you're welcome to move in. You know you always have a home here."

She winced. "I don't really want to go backward in my life." It was too late for that, but either the other ladies in the room didn't think that or they were too polite to say it, since no one said anything. She felt guilty at her mom's hurt look. "I'm sorry. I appreciate the offer, and I probably will stay a little bit if you don't mind. At least until I get back on my feet."

"Of course I don't mind!" Gita said, smiling with all the love and affection in her mother's heart at her. It made her own heart tremble and want to cry.

But she was not allowing herself the luxury of tears. Not today. That was yesterday, when she signed the papers. And realized that that part of her life was truly over. Her husband wasn't going to apologize and come back. They weren't going to attempt to sweep the ashes away and rebuild. There was no going back. It was only going forward, in a direction she hadn't anticipated, with one foot in front of the other, as painful and hard as that was.

"If there's anything I can do to help, you know I will. Tony might be able to put a word in for you at his job in Chicago if you'd like." Stacy always was a fix-it kind of person. "Or I can see if the company where I work is hiring. I haven't been paying attention, since I just do my job and spend as much time with my children as I can. You don't get this time of their lives back."

Grace nodded, although she was so far from thinking about things like that it seemed like Stacy was talking about another time and place.

"The hospital might be hiring in the administrative section. You've got plenty of experience. I can check and see and get you the information if you'd like," Jill said, and her tone was sweet and helpful.

Maybe it would be easier if her sisters had been gloating and laughing at her. Telling her that she had left with such fanfare, so prideful and arrogant, so certain she was going to take the world by the tail and slap it to the ground, reminding her of how much she thought of herself and how wrong she was.

But they hadn't, and their kindness and forgiveness of her arrogance and inconsideration was almost more than Grace could stand.

And neither of them had mentioned what she had done to Claire.

Those were all memories that belonged to yesteryear, or that's what she told herself. Although she knew with coming back to a small town, she would probably have to face them, perhaps on a daily basis for who knew how long, since small towns never forgot anything.

"You two go on. It's lunchtime for you, and I'd like to talk to Grace myself. I've not had a chance to for such a long time, and surely there are some good things that I've missed," Gita said, making a shooing motion toward Grace's sisters.

They reluctantly got up, with both of them talking about the different things that they did to help their mom. Stacy showed the pain med schedule and made sure Grace knew when the next pill was supposed to be given.

"We've been keeping her on a very strict schedule. The physical therapist said that was probably the main reason why she is doing so well. Because her pain has been managed."

Grace nodded, thinking that she'd managed to screw up everything else in her life, she would hate to screw this up too. But obviously Stacy didn't have a whole lot of faith in her ability to be able to do a good job. Either that, or she was just being Stacy, who had to control everything.

Grace figured it was probably more the latter, but it felt more like the former. That's how she felt about herself. There was no grace for the mistakes that she'd made or the problems that she brought on herself.

It wasn't too long until her sisters left, and Grace was left sitting alone beside her mother, wondering if her mom really wanted to talk to her or was just trying to shoo her other daughters out so they could take a much-needed break.

"I'm sorry you had to come back in such terrible circumstances. I have to admit I'm a little hurt that you didn't talk to me at all," Gita said, adjusting herself to a more comfortable position.

Grace sat for just a moment, just soaking in the feeling of someone caring. Why had she not wanted to come home? But then she realized she was the one who was supposed to be taking care of her mother. She got up and fluffed the pillows, tucking one closer down into her lower back.

"How's that?" she asked.

"Are you avoiding my comment?" Gita said before she said, "That's just fine."

"I suppose I am." She forced her throat to work. "Mom. I'm sorry. I guess I was just so...driven to show everyone that I could be successful. And by successful, I mean money and houses and cars and stupid stuff that doesn't matter now. Because I lost it all. It doesn't matter how successful you are; it can all come crashing down."

"I'm surprised that Lonnie turned out to be such a terrible cheater. I wouldn't have guessed." Her mom truly sounded distressed.

"I know you didn't know him very well when we got married. But I thought I did. I thought we would be together forever." She didn't know what else to say, and she shrugged her shoulders, lifting her hands, indicating that she didn't have the words. "I guess that's what everyone thinks on their wedding day."

"I don't know about everyone. But that's what I thought, too. It's hard to imagine someone cheating after saying vows in front of God."

"There's so much temptation from so many different directions. So many ways you can see other people who are cheating and enjoying it and trying to convince you that it's not that bad."

"I was concerned when you got married so young."

She had been twenty-two and hadn't graduated from college. All of her friends had slept around and weren't in a huge rush to get married. They had said exactly what her mom said, that they didn't want to get married young, but she and Lonnie were trying to live what they believed. Grace could roll her eyes over that, since she hadn't lived what she believed in any other area. She'd been so desperate for money and prestige and all the trappings of showing everyone how she'd become successful in the world's eyes that she lost sight of the things that really mattered.

"I don't think it's the age I got married. We didn't fornicate before we were married like so many of my friends. I didn't want to go that route, and Lonnie agreed." Looking back, she wondered if he had agreed, or if he had just been happy he found someone gullible enough to marry him. Or maybe he'd just been placating her and figured a wife would be a good cover for his escapades.

She'd already been through all that. The idea that he couldn't possibly have been pure like he had claimed on their wedding night, and wondering how many women he'd been with before her, and how many he'd been with during their marriage. The idea made her sick to her stomach, and she had to shove it aside. She'd spent more than enough time thinking about that, and she didn't want to have those thoughts in her head anymore at all.

"I admire that. I think you have that part right," her mom said firmly, as though she needed to reassure Grace of something.

"Thanks. I had so many other parts wrong."

"All the things that you had wrong are things that you now know are wrong, so you can learn from them."

Her mom was a big believer in positive thinking and in turning trials into stepping stones. Grace had heard that all her life. Maybe her mom was right, but sometimes a person just wanted to wallow.

Of course, wallowing wasn't a good idea. One could really spiral downward quickly.

"I think you're right, Mom. I need to do that. I just haven't figured out how." That was a problem. How did she make those things magically become the stepping stone she used to turn her life around and become...better?

"I think you've done the right thing. You're here, and there is no pressure, although you've always been very good at crafts and artsy things, and you've loved doing them, too. Plus, I need help. I didn't tell this to the girls, but I had trouble keeping up with the latest trends. I... I guess I'm a little burned out. Or maybe lonely. I'm not sure."

Grace blinked. "Mom. I didn't know."

Her mom waved a hand as though it were nothing. "I didn't want to burden anyone. Probably like you," she said with a little smile. "But you girls have been gone for so long, and it's just day in, day out, more of the same. I'm tired. Maybe it was a little bit of the pain of my hip, but I just lost my spark for life."

Grace didn't know what to say. Her mom was always happy and energetic and the kind of person who always found the positive no matter how hard it was. To hear this shocked her.

"Mom. You are the most positive person I know. I can't believe you're saying this." Did her mom need a change of scenery? Was she saying she wanted to move? Michigan winters could be brutal.

"Maybe you just need to get on a dating site and find someone."

Her mother laughed. "Maybe. I tried a couple of sites, but it's so easy to lie. I've been tempted to lie. And I'm not normally a liar. I don't know how I could trust anyone to tell the truth on those things, you know?"

Her mom was right. It was always best to have someone helping to sort truth from fiction. "You shouldn't have done that without someone knowing. Did you tell Stacy or Jill?"

"I haven't told anyone."

"You could meet a serial killer. Someone should be watching out for your welfare."

"I'm glad you're concerned. But nothing is happening, because I haven't responded to anyone. I actually took my profile down a while ago, it just... I told the Lord that if I was to get married again, I was going to have to meet the man in person, because this online stuff is just too untrustworthy."

Her mother was smart.

Grace had been duped by a man who was obviously untrustworthy, and it hadn't even occurred to her to be concerned about him lying. She just…believed Lonnie. Everything he said, she took it as gospel truth. She was such a fool.

"I'm glad to hear that, Mom. But not happy about the other stuff. You are lonely. And it sounds like you're depressed."

"I wouldn't go so far as to say I'm depressed, but I have been struggling. The idea that you might come live with me has perked me up like nothing has in a long time."

Was her mother just saying that? Did she want to take away any stigma or guilt or shame that she felt for moving backward in her life? After all, what thirty-something wanted to move back in with her mother? Unless, of course, their mother needed them. And then she would move heaven and earth to help her.

Neither one of her sisters could. They were both happily married with jobs and homes of their own. They couldn't move back in, but she could.

"Are you serious about that?"

"I am. I wasn't going to tell you any of my problems. I didn't want to burden you. But when you came and said that you didn't have anywhere else to go, it gave me hope that I haven't felt in a long time." Her mother paused. "But of course, if you find something else that makes you happy, don't feel like you have to stay with me. I'm not in that kind of situation."

"No. I know," Grace said, and she knew exactly what her mother was saying. Her mother would prefer, every day all day long, that Grace be happy. Her mother certainly would never want her living with her if Grace would prefer to do something else.

Gita was such a great example of selflessness and someone who lived to be a blessing to others.

"You think about it. You don't have to do anything. And you know I'll help you with whatever you decide, and as long as you're doing right, I'll support you however I can."

"I know, Mom. I'm sorry that I haven't been back in so long. I feel guilty about that." She felt guilty for a lot of things, stemming back long before she got married.

"Don't feel guilty. You can look back, learn from your mistakes, but don't let guilt drag you down. It will ruin your life. And you end up wasting it, instead of using it in the best way possible."

Grace nodded, knowing her mother was right.

"Now, if you don't mind, I'm going to take a little rest. The girls seem to think that they need to hover over me every second of every day, but I'm able to get up and down now without any assistance. And the only thing I needed them for was if I would fall for some reason, I might not be able to get up on my own."

"I definitely wouldn't want that to happen," Grace said.

Gita nodded. "I promise I will not try to get up if you're not here. Now, why don't you go take a rest, or maybe you can take a walk. The healing garden at the end of the road is a great place to go to try to gather your thoughts. Or you could go take a walk along the beach."

"Are you sure?"

"I am. Physical therapy comes in two hours. So, you really don't need to be back for at least three."

"All right. Although, I think I probably ought to be here when physical therapy is here so I can see what exercises you're supposed to be doing."

"Oh, trust me, Stacy's got that covered," her mom said with a slight amount of sarcasm in her voice.

Grace and Gita shared a smile over Stacy's controlling nature. Just because someone wasn't perfect didn't mean a person couldn't love them anyway. Her mother had said that to her a million times if she'd said it once.

"I think I will take a short walk, but I'll be back long before physical therapy gets here."

Her mother nodded, settling down amongst the pillows while Grace adjusted them. "I'm sorry about everything that's happened. But I'm glad you're home." She smiled as she shifted slightly and closed her eyes.

Grace had to agree. She, too, was glad she was home.

Three

Trevor Gillett finished pounding the nail in and looked around the small pasture he had just finished fencing for his dad. It wasn't too bad, considering that he was not a professional fencer. Was there even such a thing?

"You did a good job, Trevor. It only took you three years." His dad, with a smile on his face, stood beside him, looking at their handiwork.

"You look at the fence and can see that we gained experience each year."

He didn't take offense at his dad saying how long it took. It did take longer than it should have. But he needed something to do. Ever since his mother walked out on his dad, Trevor had taken it upon himself to make sure that he stopped in for regular visits. In the summer, when the weather was decent, they'd work on the fence. In the winter, and spring and fall too, they'd done other things. His dad had never been a big health enthusiast, but they did some cross-country skiing, which was really good for their health, and even took their sea kayaks out onto the lake.

The kayaking had taken Trevor a little bit of time to work up to, considering what happened when he was a teenager. It was funny how some things got pushed under the rug.

Still, he and his dad spent a lot of hours out on the lake. Hours that they could have been working on fixing the fence.

"I think we could be professionals." His dad huffed. "But I don't want to."

"Hey, it's good for your health," he said, doing what he had been doing for the last five years, and that was taking every opportunity he could to encourage his dad to be active. He had read there was a direct correlation between how active a senior was and how healthy they were during their senior years.

He didn't take every single thing that he ever read as gospel truth, but that seemed to make sense to him.

His older brother, an executive in Chicago, didn't come out much, and his sister had moved to California with her husband. They were busy having babies and building a business, and that left Trevor to take care of his dad.

"Good thing we finished. It's time for my afternoon nap," his dad said.

Trevor thought about trying to talk him out of it. Maybe taking a walk instead, but for some reason, he felt drawn to the healing garden, and he nodded instead. "I wouldn't want you to miss your nap. You'd be grumpy this evening."

"You're grumpy every evening, so I guess I'd just fit in with the crowd. Peer pressure or something like that."

"Dad, you should find a wife. Then she could put up with your grumpy rear."

"Why would I want a wife? If I got married, I wouldn't see you this evening. It's my inspiration to stay single."

Was that really true? If his dad had a wife to look after him, Trevor wouldn't have to anymore. Then he wouldn't have to come back so much. Except...

"Didn't I tell you I was going to move back?" he said, trying to say it casually, because he knew he hadn't.

"Are you serious?" his dad said, excitement on his face. He clamped a hand down on Trevor's shoulder. "That's the best news I've heard all year. In fact, that's the best news I've heard in five years."

The worst news was probably when he found the note saying that his mom had left. She hadn't even told him to his face. She'd just been bored, felt like there was more to life, and now that her kids were grown and gone, she wanted to spend time with someone who would actually do things with her.

It had gotten his dad away from the TV set, where he spent most of his retirement, up until that note. He'd lost weight and become reasonably healthy, but he hadn't gone looking for anyone else.

Trevor figured if he moved back, maybe he could help with that.

"Did you quit your job?"

He looked his dad in the eye. His dad wasn't going to be super happy with what he had to say. "I saved up enough money that I feel comfortable quitting my job, coming back here, and starting that furniture business I've always talked about."

He hadn't ever wanted to move back to Raspberry Ridge. There were too many unpleasant memories associated with it. But he hadn't figured on his dad being alone, his mom walking out, and him being the only one around to take care of him. Because of the way life went and the fact that he didn't seem to be able to find anyone himself. Really, who was he to talk to his dad about it? He hadn't put any effort into finding someone since his mom walked out, either.

A future spouse aside, he really had quit his job. He didn't have enough to live on for the rest of his life, but he had to give the furniture-making business a go.

As expected, his dad's lips turned down.

"It was a perfectly good job. Back when I was young, you didn't walk out of perfectly good jobs."

It was true, he did have a good job. And he liked it too. For the most part.

"I'm pretty sure when you were young, you didn't live so far away from your parents you couldn't help them if you needed to."

"You don't need to help me." His dad sounded gruff, but they both knew it wasn't true. Well, maybe it was technically true, but his dad didn't want to move to a retirement community.

He slid his hammer into his tool belt on his waist. "We need to do more of this kind of stuff. I don't know about you, but I really enjoy the time we get to spend together. Sometimes I almost feel like I need to thank Mom." It was true, he did feel that way, but he wasn't sure they were far enough away from the pain his dad felt that he might be able to laugh a little.

His dad chuckled, and it actually sounded like he might have been amused. "That's one way to look at it."

His dad seemed to be the kind of guy who only loved once in a lifetime. Trevor could understand that. There had only ever been one girl he had been interested in. He was one of those sorry sops who couldn't seem to get his life together after the one girl he wanted left him without an explanation, and the next thing he heard, she was hugely successful and extremely happy and making a brilliant life in some city far away.

He almost laughed out loud at that. He knew exactly where she lived. Indianapolis.

They gathered up the rest of their tools, setting them in the toolbox on the back of his truck, and then hopped in the cab.

He drove back to his dad's house, which was just outside of Raspberry Ridge, not so far that he couldn't walk to the beach anytime he wanted to, but far enough that the one parade a year they had didn't make it to his house.

"I hate to see you leave your job, but I guess you know that it'd be nice to have you hang around here." His dad didn't seem like he wanted to talk about the fact that he was growing older very much, but he was the one who brought the subject up.

"I want to move back home. You're right, it was a good job. I had nice benefits, and the work wasn't hard, just hard enough to be challenging. My boss was great, and my coworkers weren't terrible. But they don't compare to you, Dad." He grinned over at his dad.

His dad just rolled his eyes and looked back out the window. He wasn't much for talking about his feelings or anything like that. That was probably part of the reason he got in trouble with his wife. He figured their relationship was fine, and if there were any problems, he'd let her know. She, on the other hand, had tried to talk to him, and he hadn't listened. He'd said that much over the years, and it sounded like he regretted it. Trevor knew that a life lived with regrets could be pretty miserable. He wanted to live such a life that he had few regrets.

He would always wonder whether or not he should have followed Grace to Indianapolis, when she'd been so gung ho about leaving. As far as he knew, she didn't have a boyfriend that she was going to, just a job.

But Claire had been between them. Always had. And Trevor had hesitated. By the time he had things straightened out with Claire, Grace was gone.

They both got a drink when they went into the house, and Trevor washed his hands. His clothes weren't super dirty, and he decided that he'd just wear them. He'd rather take his kayak out for a ride on the lake, but he didn't want to have to unload all the boards on the back of the truck first. So a walk would have to do.

His dad went in and lay on the couch while he slipped outside, looked up at the beautiful spring day, and started down the street.

His dad hadn't asked when he was planning on quitting, and Trevor hadn't had to admit that he'd already given his two-week notice and worked it out.

He was back for good.

Part of him was excited about it, and part of him felt like he was moving backward in his life. After all, a person wasn't supposed to go back to their parents' house, back to their hometown, back to everything they'd left when they were young and full of hopes and dreams and aspirations and excitement to get it all done.

But over the years, he realized that he took more pleasure in the simple things. Family close by, a slower pace, the small-town life. And doing the woodworking he'd grown up enjoying.

He didn't know whether he could make a business out of it or not, but he should be able to spend the next ten years living with his dad, living off his savings, if he was wise, and if the woodworking business took off, he might never have to go back to work.

Who said he had to do something big with his life? He could continue to work in a suburb of Chicago, putting in eight-hour days, forty-hour weeks, and not being truly unhappy, but knowing that there was something better he could be doing.

Why would he not want to spend his dad's last days with him?

Even if it did mean going back to Raspberry Ridge where the worst memories of his life had happened.

But he didn't have to dwell on the negative. And he wasn't going to. He was going to enjoy this time with his dad, consider it bonus time, and make the best of it.

The healing garden had all the spring blooms bursting out of it and smelled amazing. He took a deep breath as he opened the little gate and walked in.

The garden was laid out in such a way that he couldn't really tell if there was anyone else there. There were two cars in the lot, but those people could be in here or down on Pebble Beach. He didn't think much about it. The garden was big enough for lots of people to have private space, but most likely, they were down on the beach.

It didn't take long before he realized at least one of the people was in the garden. She was sitting on a bench near the waterfall which happened to be his favorite spot. There was just something about hearing the water trickling by. That, and seeing the crosses which represented the children who had died over the years from Raspberry Ridge. Dominic and his wife, who designed the garden, made a little memorial for all the kids after they'd lost their own son. He thought it was a great idea, even though he couldn't really relate. He never had a child, let alone lost one, and he really didn't know what that was like.

Still, the place was calming and soothing and beautiful. But she was there first, so he nodded at the woman sitting on the bench, who looked vaguely familiar, and kept on walking.

That was one of the problems with coming back to his hometown. Everyone either knew everyone, or they looked vaguely familiar. He didn't know whether he was making it up, or whether he actually knew them. He was terrible at recognizing people, and typically other people figured out who he was first.

Chicago was a big town, and he never had that issue. But he obviously had the problem now, since the woman looked at him like she knew him. Then she looked quickly back down at the hands that were clutched together in her lap.

This was a place where people went to be soothed in their soul, not a place to remake acquaintance with people they went to high school with, so he kept on walking.

There were a couple of other spots he really enjoyed in the garden, and he ended up sitting by the tulips that were blooming profusely. They were pink and purple, and while pink was not his favorite color, he loved the deep almost black purple and the way the pink seemed to emphasize the darkness while bringing out the light.

It was done in such a way that he never got tired of looking at it and made a point to come here every year when the tulips were blooming. He sat down on the bench and thought about his dad, how many years he might have left, and whether or not he could encourage him to join a gym. Now that both of them were here together, they could drive down to Strawberry Sands in the morning, which would be the closest gym. Or he could see about buying some equipment to put in the basement of his dad's house, which was unfinished but in good enough shape that it wouldn't take much for him to turn it into a home gym.

Would that make it easier for his dad and him to stick to the workout schedule?

He hadn't figured that out when movement caught his eye, and he looked up.

It was the woman who had been sitting on the bench.

He put a pleasant look on his face, although he dreaded the interaction. She'd be offended because he didn't recognize her, he'd be embarrassed and surprised when she told him who she was.

Then, the wind caught her hair, and a microexpression blinked across her face, and suddenly everything clicked in his brain. He knew exactly who she was.

Four

Grace couldn't believe she was walking toward the man who reminded her of her high school crush, Trevor. But since she was pretty sure it was his older brother, Jimmy, she figured she'd go talk to him. Although she wasn't sure why.

She didn't want to know what was going on in Trevor's life, but after seeing the man walk by, she couldn't do anything but sit there and think about asking him about Trevor. She had put Trevor out of her mind when she got married to Lonnie. Even though Lonnie hadn't compared to Trevor. That should have been her first clue that she was making a mistake, but she had just figured that it was her first love and all of that, and those memories were bound to loom larger-than-life, even though they couldn't be accurate. After all, Trevor had just been a teenager when they'd gone out. He couldn't possibly be as special as what she remembered him as being.

And she tried to tell herself it was perfectly natural for her to be curious about him. His brother would expect her to ask about him. In fact, he'd probably think it was odd if she didn't ask. If he even recognized her, which he probably didn't.

She wasn't entirely sure it was Jimmy.

Still, as far as she knew, none of his family lived in town, except for his dad, who lived alone, since his wife had left him a few years ago. She remembered her mom talking about that.

Regardless, her feet practically went on their own accord, hunting for the man until she found him sitting at a beautiful display of tulips. She hadn't been back far enough to see it, or she might have been sitting there. She only made it to the water which she loved.

"Excuse me," she said, realizing that it was a little bit rude of her to stop and talk to someone who was obviously here for some purpose and wanted to be alone. Still, she eyed his face as he looked up with polite interest and not irritation.

At least, it was polite interest until he stood looking at her for a bit, and then something that looked a lot like horror crossed his face. She didn't expect Jimmy to be super thrilled to see her. After all, she had broken Trevor's heart and done it in a not very nice way. Anyone who loved him couldn't be faulted for not caring for her.

She hadn't thought about that, but it was too late for her to turn around and leave unless she really wanted to be rude.

"Yeah?" the man said, and he seemed a little less guarded.

"I'm sorry. You remind me of someone I used to know."

"I do?" the man said, and he seemed to have control of his expression again, because the look of horror had disappeared, and polite interest had taken its place.

"You do. I might have known your brother as a teen. Are you Jimmy Gillett?"

His brows went up, and his eyes slid away for just a second, reminding her of the way Lonnie's did every time he was going to lie to her. It was a tell she could recognize easily now, but one she had missed her entire marriage.

Finally, the man took a breath and looked back. "It's tempting to me to say that I'm Jimmy."

There. She was right. His eyes slid away because he'd been thinking about lying. She almost congratulated herself. After all, that was because of her husband cheating. Through the betrayal and the divorce and all that pain, something good came out of it. Some skills she could use in real life. Although, why she would be happy that she could tell that people were lying was beyond her. Lies did not make her happy.

"I'm sorry. You just look an awful lot like him."

"That makes sense. He's my brother."

It took her all of a second and a half for those words to sink down and for the meaning to become clear. Trevor had one brother and one sister. If this wasn't Jimmy, but Jimmy was his brother, that meant she was talking to Trevor.

Now she really did want to turn around and run away, and she didn't want to care that it would be rude. After the way she left him, that's probably what he was expecting anyway. Maybe she should just give him what he expected out of her, which was for her to be rude and unkind.

Although, during the entire time they'd been together, she'd never been anything like that. She'd been herself, more herself than she'd ever been able to be with anyone in her life before. Trevor made her feel completely at ease and had loved her for exactly who she was. She didn't feel like she had put on any show for him and had the express feeling that if she had, he wouldn't have loved her. Because it was her authenticity that he admired the most.

Most likely, she just remembered wrong. After all, first loves had a tendency to take up a lot of room in a person's brain.

She finally got her scattered wits together and said, "Then you must be Trevor." While she spoke, she was trying to figure out how she could extract herself from the situation. Could she say her mother was having an emergency? Could she pretend her phone rang? Could she send an SOS to...who? Her sisters wouldn't have any idea what she wanted, and she'd have to take her phone out to do it anyway.

Maybe he wouldn't recognize her, and she wouldn't have to say her name.

"Yes." He spoke, and his words were measured. "And you are Grace." He paused, for what, she wasn't sure. "I assume you're not still my girlfriend, even though you never officially broke up with me. You just left."

Yeah. That was exactly what she had done. It hadn't been nice. But there wasn't anything she could do to fix it now, other than apologize. "I'm sorry. You deserve so much better."

"Do I deserve an explanation now?" he asked. His question

surprised her. That had been more than a dozen years ago. Did he really want an explanation more than a decade later?

Maybe he was like her. Sometimes a person just needed closure.

"Claire."

She didn't say anything else. She figured she didn't need to.

His brows drew down, like he didn't understand. "I don't get it." He waited, and when she didn't say anything else, he continued. "Claire liked me, but I never liked her. I was always very clear about that."

"Claire accused me of stealing you. For the entire time you and I were together, Claire wouldn't talk to me."

"I remember that. You had no idea why, and I didn't either."

"She told me that I stole you from her. The only way that she would forgive me was for me to break up with you."

"I see. So you did. Because Claire meant more to you than I did."

"No!" she exclaimed. She couldn't let him think that. That wasn't right. And then she realized they would probably never see each other again. After all, it had been twelve whole years since they had graduated, and this was the first time she had seen him. He didn't live in Raspberry Ridge. If he had, she would have heard about it. So she didn't have to worry about seeing him again.

"I'm sorry I bothered you. Goodbye."

She didn't give him a chance to answer, but turned around and hurried away.

Five

S he left again. Just like she had the first time.

Trevor sat on the bench, watching as Grace hurried around the bend and out of sight.

No explanation, no idea when they might see each other again, just a quick getaway, leaving him staring after her, wishing she would come back. He didn't like that position; he'd spent too much time in it.

But she denied that her friend Claire had meant more to her than he had.

That made him feel good until he realized that it didn't mean anything, because she'd broken up with him because of Claire. He hadn't realized. He'd known Claire liked him. Known it before he and Grace got together, but Claire had never held any interest for him at all. And he highly suspected that she saw him as a conquest and hadn't been madly in love with him.

He could be wrong, but he knew how he acted when he really loved someone, and Claire had given off more of a competition vibe to him anyway.

But he didn't know anything about women. Other than they broke your heart and left without caring.

It wasn't that he put every woman in that position, but that was what had happened to him with Grace anyway.

She's still beautiful to him. Her long hair blowing in the wind, her eyes just as clear blue as they had always been, and while she didn't have the stick straightness of her teenage years, she looked like she was athletic and healthy.

Still not interested in him. That was the conclusion he came to. That she hadn't wanted him anymore and hadn't figured out how to tell him. One would think he would get the memo and be okay with it. Realize that some things just weren't meant to be. And Grace and him were one of those things.

He pushed off the bench, no longer interested in enjoying the beauty of the garden, although he did take one last glance at the tulips as he walked away from them. They were gorgeous, so pretty, and so faithful. Year after year, they came up and bloomed with dependability no matter what was going on around them. Whether the winter had been brutal or better than usual. Whether the spring was rainy or sunny or something in between. They were there. That's what he had wanted. Someone who was going to be there for him, no matter what.

He didn't know why he'd always been so stuck on Grace. It was obvious that she wasn't going to be there for him. She couldn't stick around long enough to have a conversation with him. Long enough for him to challenge her on her no, because she had thought more of Claire than she had Trevor. Otherwise, she wouldn't have broken up with him.

And he would have left it at that, except with all her faults, there was one fault that Grace did not have. She was not a liar.

He left the garden and walked by the first house on the street, where Homer and Skyler lived with their four children. His mother had passed away the year before, and the whole town had taken it rather hard. Everyone had good memories of Mrs. Aiken, but Skyler, Homer's wife, was a sweet lady who slid into the role of the heart of Raspberry Ridge with little effort.

"Nice day." He nodded as he passed their porch, where Skyler sat with three other ladies, open Bibles on their knees. Bible study must have commenced since he had walked to the garden.

"It sure is," Skyler said, smiling at him and nodding. The other ladies greeted him as well, and he figured they were doing Bible study while her kids were in school. Interesting the things he didn't know, for as much time as he spent around town.

They didn't do more than say a few words to him about the weather, and he didn't stop.

With this many unmarried women in Raspberry Ridge, he couldn't believe his dad hadn't been able to find someone.

Probably it was because of what Trevor had figured earlier, and that was that he was a one-woman man and would never love anyone but Trevor's mother.

But none of that was what he really wanted to think about. He'd seen Grace. For the first time in more than a decade, he'd seen the woman he couldn't forget. It was crazy, because he knew her as a teenager. She was different. She had to change, just as he had. He certainly wasn't the boy that he used to be. Still, he hadn't felt that soul-deep rightness in more than a decade, and it was all he could do to not ask his dad about her immediately when he walked in the door. But he was preoccupied and seemed to be tidying up.

Tidying up was something his mom had done. It was odd to see his dad with the broom and dustpan.

"I can help you with that," he said, taking the dustpan and holding it so his dad could sweep the pile of dirt that he'd gathered up onto it.

"Thanks. Considering you made half of this, it's only fitting that you should help clean it up."

He had no idea when the last time his dad swept was, but he refrained from commenting.

Unfortunately, he didn't refrain from saying the next thing. "You didn't tell me that Grace Honea was back in town."

"That's not her last name anymore, and I didn't know it."

"You mean you didn't hear it when you went to Bible study this morning?" That was where his dad got all of the juicy gossip.

He shouldn't think that. He knew that they really did study the Bible, but they also shared what was going on in their lives, which was basically what was going on in Raspberry Ridge.

"Come to think of it, maybe I did," his dad said, making Trevor want to strangle him. Surely his dad knew he would have been interested in that information. Maybe he had, but it wasn't exactly something that came up easily in conversation.

"Pastor Irving said something about it." His dad scratched his head and then held his hand out for the dustpan. Trevor gave it over without thinking about it.

"I can't believe you didn't think to tell me."

"Why would I do that?" his dad asked, and Trevor couldn't tell whether he was playing innocent, or whether he really didn't know. After all, how many people spent twelve years mooning over their high school girlfriend?

"I guess... Just... If you hear anything else about her, I'd like to know." There. He might have shown his hand to his dad, but it wasn't like he was confessing undying love for her or anything. He really was curious. Where had she been? What was she doing? Would she have to stay?

He shook his head at that last one. She was married. Most likely happily married and living in Indianapolis. That was why he hadn't tried to contact her.

"Never mind. I don't need to hear anything."

Maybe it was his tone, or maybe it was his words, but his dad paused with the dustpan hovering over the garbage can.

"Why not? You just said you did. That's an awful short span to be changing your mind."

"She's married. And I don't need to know."

"Actually, I'm not sure she is." His dad stared down at the garbage can before dumping the contents of the dustpan in and tapping it gently on the edge. He allowed the lid to the can to fall back down and then walked over to put the broom behind the pantry door where he kept it.

"Wait. What? You don't think she's married?" Had he heard wrong? Had he been thinking she was married all these years when she actually wasn't? He couldn't believe it. Surely he hadn't been that wrong. He was sure he had heard she was married. He'd seen her in Indianapolis with a ring on her finger laughing with a man at an outside table at some swanky restaurant.

Not that he had been stalking her or anything, he just...asked a few questions, made a few inquiries here and there, and then got a little lucky when he was in Indianapolis.

She'd looked so happy. So beautiful. So completely on top of the world, and that wasn't the way she had been when she was with him. Or at least, maybe she had been happy, but she had seemed so...successful. Whatever. He couldn't push into that world and didn't want to. She was married; she was off limits. He had never tried to find her again.

"I don't know. Just from what they were saying at Bible study today, I got the impression that she wasn't." His dad finally answered him after several minutes of silence.

"I see. I guess I could ask around."

"I take it you're interested?"

"No. I'm not." That wasn't a lie. He said it, feeling like he was telling the truth. What they had was long over. Sure, he carried a torch in his heart for his high school flame, but the woman that the girl had become was not someone he knew. And he definitely was not interested in someone who was married or someone who was separated. There needed to be a finality, and even then, he wasn't necessarily interested in someone who got divorced just because she wasn't happy in her marriage. The only reason God gave for divorce was adultery. Otherwise, it was wrong.

Plus, there were an awful lot of secrets and tragedy sitting between Grace and him. Sometimes he forgot about it, because he pushed it out of his mind, but the fact remained that Grace most likely wanted to have nothing to do with him. And if he was smart, he would feel the same. He would want nothing to do with her either. There were too many things that were buried that would get exposed, and that was not a wise trail. Definitely not one he wanted to go down.

Six

"I thought I might go with you today." Don looked up in surprise as he picked up his Bible from the coffee table in the living room.

He didn't want his son to go to Bible study today of all days.

"Do you think you'd enjoy it? Most of us are retired, and I'm not sure that you'd feel comfortable with so many oldies."

His son gave him a look. Rightfully so, because why wouldn't he be happy that his son wanted to go to Bible study with him? Of course he was. He was thrilled. He loved going with his son anywhere. He was proud of his boys, both of them, and his daughter too, but Trevor had a sensitivity and caring about him that the other two either didn't have or were too busy to show.

"Dad, if you don't want me to go with you, I don't have to."

"You know I do, son."

He had planned to make a stop before he got to Bible study, but he couldn't make it if his son was with him. Their conversation yesterday had given him an idea, one that five years ago he would never even have thought of or considered, but he hated seeing his son miserable, and yesterday he'd been interested in someone—a woman—for the first time since Don could remember. He wasn't going to let that opportunity slip by him. Even if it meant that the thing that he'd always wanted, one of his kids to come live with him, wasn't going to happen. He wasn't so selfish that he didn't want his son to have a beautiful and full marriage, like he had had. At least until Emma had left him.

"All right then. For a minute there, I was starting to think that you were offended that I wanted to go to Bible study with you." His son sounded perplexed but not suspicious, which was good.

Now, how was he going to be able to get out of walking with him? He didn't absolutely have to make the side trip that he wanted to, but...

Then, an idea occurred to him.

"If you don't mind, I'm leaving early. I wanted to go to the healing garden. This is the five-year anniversary of your mother leaving."

His son stood there, his mouth open, staring at him. Don lifted a shoulder, gave a little expression as though to say what could he expect, and then looked down.

In his head, he was frantically trying to remember what day she actually left. If he couldn't remember, surely Trevor didn't remember either, right?

He wasn't sure, but he hoped that was accurate. He remembered it was sometime in the spring, but he was drawing a blank on the exact day. He'd been devastated, completely blindsided, and totally out of it. In fact, he didn't think that he actually rejoined the land of the living for at least a year, maybe two.

"Oh. I'm sorry. I...forgot, I guess." Trevor looked abashed that he had been so insensitive on such an important day.

"No need to apologize. I just...wanted to leave a little early."

"That's fine. You go ahead and go. I'll come a little later. First, I'm going to put some pepper jack cauliflower in the slow cooker. We'll have something to look forward to when we get back."

"It's our favorite," Don said, wondering again how he had gotten such a carbon copy of himself in his son. The other two kids were a nice mix of Emma and him together. In fact, looking at his daughter he almost saw more Emma and very little of him. She had his stubborn streak, and that was pretty much it. But with Trevor, they had the same taste, the same interests, the same personality. He could almost tell exactly what Trevor was thinking before Trevor even opened his mouth. He could pretty much say the sentences Trevor was going to say. He didn't want to be arrogant and say that he was able to know everything about his son, but sometimes it seemed that way to him.

"I'll meet you there," he said as he grabbed his Bible and walked out. Skyler had a Bible study for ladies in the afternoon, but Homer hosted the Bible study that Pastor Irving did in the morning for not just ladies but anyone. They didn't have to be retired, although that's usually who went.

Why did people wait until they were old to get serious about following the Lord? That's what he had done. It had taken his wife leaving before he had developed the walk with God that he had now. Sure, he'd always been a fairly decent Christian, at least in his eyes, but he hadn't been serious. Not until Emma left, and he realized that his Christianity and salvation were totally dependent on him and not on who he was married to. More times than he could count, he let Emma go to church for both of them. He wished he could go back and take it back. Maybe she would stay. Although, that was probably just wishful thinking. He didn't think that there was anything that he could have done that would have made her stay. After all, it was her lack of character that had allowed her to leave in the first place. If she had had a good character, she wouldn't have even considered leaving her husband.

He wanted to look behind him as he left, to make sure Trevor wasn't watching, but he didn't. He could go in the right direction, then take a side street and double back, cross Geraldine's yard, and show up at Gita's house.

He and Gita had talked a little bit over the years, but not much. She had been friends with Emma, had probably been just as shocked as he was when Emma left. Although, come to think of it, maybe she had known all along that Emma was going to leave. Maybe Emma had confided in her friend, and...

He wasn't going to think like that. He couldn't. He needed Gita to help him. And he wasn't going to get himself all worked up thinking that maybe she knew his wife was leaving before he did and she did nothing to stop it.

What did he expect her to do? Kidnap Emma and tie her up in her basement and then call him? What would he have done then?

No, Emma left of her own free will, because of her lack of character.

Gita had nothing to do with it, and while he could have been a better husband, that wasn't why she left. Maybe she wasn't happy. Maybe she knew he could have been better. Maybe she wanted more romance or less TV or more money or whatever, but it didn't matter. If she was willing to make vows before God and then break them when she wasn't satisfied with whatever was going on in her marriage, that was on her. Not him.

Still, there were things he had learned from that. Like you couldn't make someone stay. Like he couldn't go back and redo things that he wished he could, so he'd better do them right the first time. And that a man got awfully lonely when he didn't have his lifetime mate beside him.

That's why he was going to Gita's house. Trevor had to be lonely, and he had been more interested in Grace than he had been in anyone for a long time. Don had every intention in the world of helping him out.

Because maybe his own marriage had failed, but that didn't mean he didn't believe in the institute of marriage, or want that for himself, but most especially for the son that he loved with all of his heart and soul.

Seven

Gita lifted her head. Was that a knock on her door? Who could be stopping in to visit at this time of morning?

She would have to answer the door herself, since she had given Grace the grocery list, and Grace was making a quick run to the store, while Jill and Stacy had left early that morning after breakfast.

Gita had promised Grace that she would not get up out of her chair the entire time she was gone. There was a grocery store down in Blueberry Beach, and it would be at least two hours until Grace got back.

But she couldn't not open the door.

"I don't think it's locked. Come on in." She used the loudest voice she could. Hopefully whoever had knocked had heard her and would let themselves in. Grace might have locked the door, but Gita never did. After all, it was Raspberry Ridge. Who was she locking the door against?

"Did you say to come in?" a gruff male voice said as the door squeaked. She assumed he must have pushed it open far enough for him to get his head in so he could ask.

"I did. I'm sorry I can't get up. Well, I can, but I promised my daughter I wouldn't."

"It's funny how the rules change as we get older, and the kids start calling the shots," the man said as the door squeaked again. She assumed he was opening it and walking in.

"Yeah. But especially now since I just had a hip replacement and my daughters are taking care of me. Well, daughter, now that my other two girls left. Come on in," she said again as she waited for a body to fill the doorway. The voice sounded familiar, but she couldn't quite place it.

Then, as the man appeared, she recognized him.

"Don. What are you doing here?" she asked, and then she realized it wasn't a very welcoming statement. "I mean, come on in. Sit down. I'd offer you some refreshments or food, but like I said, I just had a hip replacement and I'm not allowed up."

Gita didn't know Don super well, but she saw him at church occasionally. He'd gone a lot more since his wife left, but sometimes she went to church down in Blueberry Beach so she could see Stacy, and other times she went to church with Jill, just so that they could see each other. So now she supposed that she was the one who seemed to be not faithful to the Lord's house.

"I don't have a lot of time, but I had something I wanted to run by you that is going to seem very...odd and perhaps outside of your comfort zone."

"All right. I'm intrigued," she said. Things that were outside of her comfort zone were right up her alley at this stage of her life.

He grinned at her, enjoying her sense of humor, she supposed, or else enjoying the thought of whatever it was that he wanted to run by her.

He finished coming into the room and sat down on the edge of the chair beside her so they could look at each other. He didn't slide back, or look comfortable, but rather propped his forearms on his knees and steepled his hands together.

"I can't believe I'm here, thinking about this. I think I've watched too many sappy movies since my wife left."

"There are a lot of sappy movies on TV. But there's other stuff on TV too. You could probably turn the channel."

He grinned a bit. "Maybe I gave you the impression that I didn't like sappy movies. That was incorrect."

"Oh," she said, realizing that he hadn't been saying what she thought he'd been saying at all. She chuckled. "I like it. Go on."

"I have to be fast. So I'm just going to jump into it. My son Trevor dated your daughter back in the day."

"He was her one true love, I think. She ended up getting married to someone else, but I don't think that person ever measured up to the standard that Trevor set." Perhaps that wasn't her info to share, but Don wasn't the kind of man who got news then ran all over town with it.

"That's interesting. I mentioned it because my son ran into your daughter yesterday, and he asked me about her. I didn't realize she was back in town, and I couldn't give him any information on her, which, in hindsight, is probably good. But I love my son, and I can tell that he's still interested. I was wondering if you might be interested in playing matchmaker with me. That is if your daughter is available?"

"I found out yesterday she is divorced. It's final, but it's been over a year since the inciting incident, I guess you could call it. So, yes, that was a long, roundabout way of saying that yes, she is available."

"Nice."

"How would we play matchmaker?" She'd never even considered doing something like this before. Ever. But she wasn't too old to try new things. The thought made a spark of excitement go through her.

"Well, here's where things get a little dicey for you and me. I was thinking if you and I pretend to be interested in each other and start spending time together...or we could have a fake relationship. Or whatever it is. It happens all the time in sappy movies. Anyway, in the movies, two people play matchmaker by faking a relationship, then their kids are forced to spend time together and they end up falling in love."

"I see. Maybe you have been watching too many of them. That's probably the clue, when you start to think it will work in real life." She chuckled. And then she said, "It appears that I've watched too many of the same movies, because I am totally on board with this. Let's pretend to have a relationship so that our kids will have to spend time together. Because my daughter is here taking care of me, and she's a captive audience."

"And my son just informed me that he quit his job and he wanted to move in with me. So he is a captive audience as well."

They stared at each other, then they each cracked a smile, and Gita had to admit that she was glad he had shown up. He had made her somewhat boring life all of a sudden a lot more interesting.

"All right. I think I better give you my phone number. And we can start texting. That's what all the kids do nowadays, isn't it?"

"Maybe I don't want to be a modern woman. Maybe I am old-fashioned and I want you to write letters and send them by snail mail. And I want flowers and candy and serenades out by my porch."

"Wow. I'd forgotten how much work courting really was. No wonder the kids are doing it differently nowadays. At least from the male perspective, I can say I understand."

"I was kidding," Gita said, although she really did love the old-fashioned courting much better than she liked the newfangled stuff of modern life. It was all about hookups and quick fixes and easy and fast. She kind of thought that maybe the older generation had it right.

Don looked at her like he was maybe thinking about what she said. "I suppose if I'm getting the lady to agree with me about being in a fake relationship, I ought to be willing to put some effort into it."

"No. There's no need for that at all. If you were in a real relationship, maybe." She batted her eyes at him. And then she grew serious immediately. "But we should know a little bit about each other. I mean, we can learn as we spend more time together, that would be the way it would happen in a normal relationship. But we have to know enough that we know we like each other and want to court."

"Good point. First thing we should know is our phone numbers." He got up from his chair and came over. She grabbed her phone and rattled off her number. He punched it in and then sent her a text.

"All right. Step one is taken care of. I suppose step two is figuring out how we met."

"At church? That's the truth. We just didn't hit it off like maybe someone might assume we did, since we're now courting."

She giggled a little. This was too fun and too funny. "All right. I think the truth is always better than a lie. So we'll just tell the truth. And we'll let people infer whatever they want to, even if it's wrong."

Their eyes twinkled at each other. She got the feeling that Don was having just as much fun as she was.

"My wife left five years ago, and I wasn't really interested in dating anyone until you came along. In church," he added with a wink.

"My husband passed away more than a decade ago, and I wasn't interested in anyone until you came along. In church." She winked back at him.

They giggled, almost like teenagers. She hadn't had this much fun in ages.

"I'll text you some of my hobbies. You can send me yours and any other info I should know, and I'll start writing you a letter to send via snail mail. I'm not much for serenading, but I do have a guitar, and back in the day, I used to play. Maybe I can brush up on a love song."

"Oh goodness. I wouldn't want you to go out of your way like that for me."

"I want to. Fake dating or no, I'm going to do right by the lady."

"All right then. My favorite music is hymns. Maybe that'll make it a little easier for you. You don't have to sing me some kind of sappy rock 'n' roll garbage."

"Hey, watch what you're calling garbage," he said, but she knew he was kidding because he was smiling.

"If you want to impress the lady, make it a hymn." She blinked her eyes at him and tried to simper. She'd never been a simperer, and she had a feeling she failed miserably. But maybe he seemed to be a little bit affected by it, because his eyes dropped to her lips.

Maybe he was doing that on purpose. Maybe that was part of courting, even if they were doing it in a fake way.

Maybe she should admire his muscles. But he had a button-down on over a white T-shirt, and a vest over the top of that. She really couldn't see any muscles.

But he did have nice facial hair.

"Your facial hair is outstanding," she said, and then she rolled her eyes. "I think maybe I haven't watched enough of those sappy movies. That was a pathetically terrible attempt at flirting."

"I actually thought it was really good. So you admire my beard, huh?"

"Oh, greatly."

"And I admire your eyes," he said with just the barest pause before the word "your," like he was desperately trying to find something on her that he could admire. She almost thought that maybe he was going to say something inappropriate and saved it at the last moment.

But surely not. He was an upstanding, upright man and would not be tempted to ogle anything that he shouldn't. Right?

Well, she didn't know men very well, but if she knew them at all, he was probably more than tempted, and he was probably ogling when she wasn't looking. But she certainly would not lay any blame at his feet, because she was doing a little looking herself. She just would not call it ogling.

"All right. I'm supposed to be at the healing garden, because I told my son it was the five-year anniversary of my wife walking out on me, and so I needed to leave early for Bible study."

"Oh," she said, feeling instantly bad. "I'm so sorry."

"I'm not sure it's actually today or not. It was a...cloudy time for me. It might be true though. Because she did leave in the spring."

"Oh. Well, if you ever had trouble remembering her birthday or your anniversary, she probably would be very happy to note that you have trouble remembering the date that she left, too."

He apparently hadn't thought of that before, because he guffawed quite loudly.

It made her feel witty, that he was laughing at her attempted joking. Which made her smile even bigger.

"You know, I wasn't sure this was a good idea when I came to ask you. I was only thinking that I really wanted to help my son. He's been stuck on your daughter since grade school. And I know what it's like to be stuck on someone. Just never want to look anywhere else. But maybe this will be good for me too. And maybe... Maybe you'll get some kind of benefit out of it as well." He backed away, looking at her like he was thinking, and she really would have loved to know what was going on in his head.

Had she just agreed to...fake date this man? She should be appalled at herself, but she was having trouble wanting to do anything but laugh.

This was going to be so fun. And who knew? Maybe their children would find each other and be happy, and it would be worth it.

There was a part of her that almost asked the question, *but what about you? Where is this going to leave you?*

But she felt like she was old enough and wise enough and had been through enough to take a chance like this. She didn't know Don very well, but he was a good man, and he wasn't going to do anything untoward toward her, so she didn't have to worry about that, and she certainly was going to treat him with respect as well.

"Maybe you can come over for dinner sometime," she said as he looked like he was getting ready to turn around and leave. "In fact, I'd like it if you would," she said, kind of pretending to be shy and uncertain but just mostly allowing what she actually felt to come out.

He grinned. "I've got some pepper jack cauliflower in the crockpot that I would really love to share with you. Maybe, if you would be interested in getting together later today?"

"I would definitely be interested. Anytime."

They grinned at each other, and she figured they probably did look like lovesick fools.

"My son lives with me. I would probably have to bring him along. I hope that wouldn't inconvenience you."

"Oh, not at all. And my daughter lives with me, so she'll probably be joining us. I hope that doesn't upset you?"

She had the strangest urge to giggle at their little pretend drama. Was this a comedy? She wasn't sure. She supposed it should be a love story, but she was having too much fun. It had to be a romcom. "I've always wanted my own romcom. I feel like I'm living it now."

His eyes twinkled. "I'm happy to be the leading man in your romcom."

They grinned before he put up a hand and waved, and then walked toward the door. She was a little bit relieved. She didn't want Grace to come back before he left. She was going to have to figure out how to tell Grace that she had a man in her life and had for a while, she wasn't sure how long, and somehow she managed to not tell her other two daughters, and...he hadn't been there to help when she had her hip operation.

It would be okay. She could say they just started dating. That's how they'd handle that.

Humming to herself, she lifted the book that she'd been reading back up off the coffee table where she set it when he'd knocked on the door, but it was a while before she got back into her story.

Eight

"You have one?" Grace asked, shocked that her mother had just said she had a boyfriend. But... Why hadn't anyone told her about it?

"We just recently became official," her mother said, and Grace narrowed her eyes at the unfamiliar language coming out of her mother's mouth.

"You've become official?"

"You know. Facebook official?"

"You're Facebook official?"

"No. I'm not on Facebook, but if we were, it would be Facebook official."

"I'm confused."

Any rational person in her position would have been confused. What in the world was her mother saying?

"Anyway, he's coming over for lunch, and he's bringing his slow-cooker pepper jack cauliflower. I was hoping that we could make sandwiches to go along with it." Her mother looked a little bit ashamed. "You. I was hoping that *you* could make sandwiches. I can get up, but I'm not supposed to be on my feet that long."

"And I wouldn't want you to be. Of course I can make sandwiches for your...boyfriend." She stumbled over the word "boyfriend." Stumbled badly.

Her mother with a boyfriend?

But wasn't she just thinking yesterday that she wanted her to have someone? She didn't want her mother spending the rest of her life alone. Of course she didn't. But...this was shocking. She supposed she hadn't put enough thought into how that was actually going to feel. How it was going to look. How it was going to affect her. Her mother... with a boyfriend. That sounded so...weird.

"You're going to love him. And maybe you should make a couple of extra sandwiches because his son is moving in with him, and he might be coming along for lunch."

"His son? Do I know him?"

"Oh, I don't know. When they get here, you'll figure out whether you do or not."

That sounded odd. Why didn't her mom just tell her whether she knew him or not? Which would mean whether or not they grew up in Raspberry Ridge. If they lived there, Grace knew them. It was as simple as that. Unless they'd moved in after she moved out. But Raspberry Ridge was a kind of town where everyone knew everyone else.

Her mother was acting strange for sure.

Maybe she was a little bit embarrassed because she had a boyfriend. A boyfriend, her mother. It was so...strange.

She went to the kitchen and put the sandwiches together, shaking her head and trying to process the idea of her mother with someone the whole time. She tried to focus on whether she should cut them in some kind of fancy way, or whether this was just a casual lunch with her... boyfriend. Her mother had gone into the bathroom, and it occurred to Grace that she might be fixing her hair and making herself look cute for her...boyfriend. Wow, as much as she was happy for Mom, and excited too, it was such a weird thing. Her mom with a boyfriend.

Once her mom came out of the bathroom, she would demand to know who they were. After all, she might want to skip out. There weren't a whole lot of people in town that she didn't get along with, but...no one was coming to mind that she wouldn't want to eat lunch with, except Trevor.

And that wasn't because she didn't like him. It was because…why? She felt uncomfortable? He brought back memories she would rather not think about? Or was she afraid that her feelings for him had never really died? That if she spent too much time around him, she'd end up chasing him and begging him to take her back?

She'd apologized for what she'd done to him. She could at least think of that and be somewhat happy, even though she was greatly ashamed at the way that she treated him.

She could have, and should have, done a lot better by him.

"What time are they—" She didn't get the question out before there was a knock on the door.

She put the last sandwich down on a tray and left it on the kitchen counter before she walked into the living room to answer the door.

She almost closed the door the second she opened it. Trevor and his dad stood there looking at her. Trevor looked distinctly uncomfortable.

"You're my mom's new boyfriend?"

"New?" Trevor said before his dad could utter a word. He looked at his dad. "You told me you guys have been together for a while."

"Well, it's kind of ambiguous. When you get to be our age, I think new can also mean a while."

Grace narrowed her eyes. "My mom said this was new."

"It is," Don said, nodding his head, as though the faster he nodded, the more true his statement became.

"But you told me a while."

"That's right," Gita said from behind Grace.

Grace narrowed her eyes even further. "Is your father dealing with Alzheimer's?" she asked, lifting her brows at Trevor. It seemed that Don and Gita couldn't get their story straight, and one of them could be dealing with the mental issues that came with age.

"I'm perfectly fine."

"He's perfectly fine," Gita said.

Meanwhile, Trevor shrugged his shoulders. "He could be. This has been…very sudden." He closed his mouth, and then he said under his breath, "To say the least."

"We just didn't want to tell everyone right away," Gita said, walking forward and hugging Don, who, unless Grace missed her guess, looked surprised and then excited. He enthusiastically hugged her back.

Grace looked at Trevor. Trevor raised his brows and looked right back at her. They needed to talk.

"Why don't you two come in, and you can get settled at the table." She noticed that Trevor was holding a crockpot, which must have been the cauliflower her mom had been talking about.

"How about you follow me into the kitchen, Trevor, and we'll deal with the cauliflower." *And whatever else we need to deal with concerning our parents*, she added silently, but Trevor was going to hear it as soon as they were alone.

Don and Gita looked at each other like they had just won the lottery and were super excited and couldn't figure out exactly what they wanted to do with all their money.

That confused Grace even more. After all, if they really wanted to be alone, it wasn't like they had chaperones and they couldn't be. She couldn't figure out why else they'd be excited for her and Trevor to leave them alone while they went into the kitchen.

As soon as Trevor stepped through the door, she closed it behind him and then turned on him.

"What is going on?" She put her hands on her hips and then realized that she was attacking him, when he looked as confused as she did. He turned around and gazed at her.

He set the crockpot on the counter and then lifted his hands in the air in innocence. "I have no idea. My dad blindsided me with this about five minutes ago. It was almost like he was afraid to tell me." He sighed. "I don't feel like I'm that scary."

She scoffed. "I know it's taken me a little bit to get used to the idea... Who am I kidding? I'm not used to the idea, and my mom dropped this bombshell on me about thirty minutes ago." She crossed her hands over her chest. "I didn't mean to sound like I was attacking you. I just...am totally surprised. Although I can't say I'm upset. I've been thinking for a while how nice it would be for my mom to find someone. Back when we were younger, my sisters and I tried to ask her why she wasn't dating or trying to find someone after Dad died. And she just wasn't interested. So, on the one hand, I'm really happy, but on the other, I wasn't expecting this. Like a fully formed relationship sprung on me. I mean, they hug each other."

"Yeah. I was afraid he was going to smack her on the lips, and I wanted to get out of there as fast as I could. This is going to take a little bit of...time for me to get used to the idea of my dad kissing someone other than my mom."

"I remember my mom and dad kissing. And at the time, it was embarrassing. Looking back, I think it was sweet, but now...her kissing someone else? That's weird. Even if it is your dad. No offense."

"None taken. I'm the same way. Kissing my mom, yes, and I understand why he does not want to be kissing my mom anymore, considering that she left him. So that's not hard either. But what's tough is the idea of someone else. Just not sure how I feel about that."

"I feel good about it, but it makes me uncomfortable and I feel a little off-balance. My mom is a rock. She's happy, and positive, and always making sure to do the right thing. I can depend on her. But this is new. It's different, and it feels slightly disorienting." She didn't know how else to explain it, but Trevor looked like he understood exactly what she was saying.

He nodded. "We just have to get used to this."

"In the meantime, we can get that cauliflower out and put it in a bowl and take it to the table."

"Can I help with anything?"

"There's iced tea in the fridge. Maybe you can get it out and take it to the table."

"Sure," he said.

It didn't take long for her to scoop the cauliflower out of the crockpot and put it in a serving bowl. She carried it to the table and saw everyone else was already sitting down waiting for her.

"Shall we say grace?" Don asked, sounding confident and in charge, even as he exchanged a shy glance with her mother.

Grace couldn't help it, her eyes met Trevor's, and they exchanged a look before she bowed her head and said her own silent prayer, that her mother wasn't going crazy. After all, this was really fast.

"So," her mom said after they had passed the cauliflower around and everyone had gotten a sandwich. "Donnie and I have been talking, and we were hoping that the two of you would agree to be our chaperones. We want to set a good example for our families and for the town, and we don't want to do anything inappropriate. But we'd like to take our relationship to the next level."

"And we can't do that without a chaperone. Because, like Gita Baby said, we want to be a good example, and we also want to please the Lord in everything we do."

Gita Baby? Grace couldn't help it. Her eyebrows shot up, and it almost felt like they bounced off the ceiling.

If she'd been looking at herself, she probably would have laughed, but the fact that he had a nickname for her mother already... This was more serious than she thought. Relationships where folks were tossing nicknames around were the kind of relationships that ended in marriage.

She glanced at Trevor. Maybe he had the same expression on his face after her mom had called his dad Donnie. She'd never heard anyone call him that before. From the look on Trevor's face, neither had he.

Their parents certainly were settling into a familiarity with each other that was...well, it would be endearing if it weren't so flipping scary.

"I think I need you two to just kinda calm down a little bit, because this is really hard to get used to. Did Stacy and Jill know about this?" she asked her mother, hoping she sounded reasonable and not negative or angry.

Her mother blinked and then looked at Don. Or Donnie, as she was calling him. "I can't remember whether I said anything to them or not."

"I don't think you did, Gita Baby. We decided that we didn't want to say anything until we were sure about each other."

There was a seductive, sexy tone in Don's tone that made Grace blink. He was an old man, well, into his sixties, and there he was sounding sexy? So weird. Her mom was simpering like she heard that note, and it was working on her instead of grossing her out.

"And that was today?" Trevor said. Grace wasn't sure, but there seemed to be a note of disbelief in his tone.

"Yes. We text, you know," Gita said, lifting up her phone as though she needed to prove it.

"But we don't send naked pictures," Don said, and Grace felt relief and was also surprised at how quick she wanted to throw up.

She tried not to let either feeling show. After all, she was the one who made the sandwiches, and she wouldn't want anyone to think the sandwiches were turning her stomach.

"All right. I'll agree to be one of your chaperones, but I have to let you know that if you're going to be sending naked pictures, you're going to lose phone privileges."

"I don't think so," Don started to say, and then his lips clamped closed as he glanced at Gita. "Yes. Actually, that's exactly what you need to do. If you catch anything inappropriate, you definitely need to take my phone."

Gita and Don exchanged a glance that Grace could not read. She moved her gaze to Trevor and could tell that he wasn't quite buying things either. There was something fishy going on. But she couldn't put her finger on it, and she wasn't completely sure it wasn't just the fact that her mother had a boyfriend, and that was making her feel weird.

"So, what made you two decide you wanted to be together?" Trevor asked, and he sent a glance at Grace that she couldn't interpret. She thought maybe he was saying that they could ask some questions and try to trip them up and figure out what exactly was going on. But Grace wasn't entirely sure that there would be any tripping up going on. After all, it wasn't like the two of them were teenagers and trying to get away with anything. They flat-out asked them to chaperone them, and Don even said that if they found anything inappropriate in his phone, he wanted it to be taken away. So, it was only awkward because it was unexpected. Not because they were doing anything wrong.

Still, she understood what Trevor was probably feeling, and she could help him, even if she didn't think that he was going to get anywhere.

"Yes, tell us your story," she said.

"Last week—"

"Two months ago—"

Gita tilted her head and gave Don a look that could only be described as simpering. "Why don't you tell them, darling?"

"As you wish, Gita Baby," Don answered.

It was going to take her a very long time, probably a hundred years or more, to get used to hearing her mother called Gita Baby. She wanted to snatch the words from the air and shove them back in Don's mouth. Her mother was not Gita Baby.

Except, Don was her boyfriend, and he could call her whatever he wanted to, and she seemed to like it. Which was really odd. What kind of normal person enjoyed being called Gita Baby?

"We've seen each other around the church. We said hi, we noticed each other. You know, the way things go sometimes. And then…" It looked like he puttered out and wasn't quite sure what to say.

Her mom—Gita Baby—picked up the slack for him. "I admired his gorgeous facial hair. He just looks so dashing."

"And I admired her…uh, armpits, uh, that didn't have any hair," Don said. Either he had a hard time giving compliments or a hard time thinking up lies on the spot.

"You also said you liked my smile, Donnie," her mother said, and *good night*, her mother actually batted her eyes like she was fifteen instead of sixty.

"I do. It's gorgeous, Gita Baby."

Maybe it was the way he said it, more than the name itself. It was almost like he added a sexy emphasis on "baby," saying it in a deeper, sultry voice that reminded her of a stripper popping out of a cake. Not that she had ever seen such a thing.

Although, she did make a mental note to ask Trevor if his dad had ever popped out of a cake before. An affirmative answer could quite possibly shed some light on things.

She hated to be untrusting, but she had trouble with their answers. They seemed…contrived almost. Although, the nicknames were a nice touch. She and her husband had never had nicknames for each other. Maybe that was why their relationship was doomed from the start.

In her next relationship, she was going to have nicknames. That was a given.

"I'm simply tired of being alone," her mother said, and that sounded honest. "We enjoy each other's company, and we have a lot of fun together."

"Gita Baby makes me laugh," Don said, and they shared such a tender glance that Grace almost felt like she was intruding and that maybe she should look away. "I haven't laughed like I have with her in a really long time."

"But if you guys aren't comfortable being our chaperones—" Gita started, but then Don finished for her.

"Even though we raised you, paid for your food and shelter for the first eighteen or twenty years of your life, taught you not to defecate in public, gave you wisdom, and spent all of our spare time, money, and energy on you in order to give you a chance of succeeding in the world… You know, if you don't feel like you can chaperone us, that's totally up to you."

Grace found herself trying hard not to laugh, although Don sounded completely serious. If this was the kind of guilt trip that Trevor had to deal with growing up, it was a wonder he spent any time at all with his dad. Although, there wasn't anything his dad said that wasn't true.

"You're right, Dad. I owe you. I'll happily chaperone, although obviously I can't speak for Grace."

"I'll happily chaperone too, as long as there's no naked pictures. That is a definite no go for me."

"There will be no naked pictures. He was just telling you that there weren't going to be any naked pictures. Weren't you, darling?" her mom said, looking over and simpering at Don again.

The simpering was going to take Grace a really long time to get used to.

"That's right, Gita Baby."

Grace looked down at her plate and her uneaten sandwich and the cauliflower that smelled amazing. She hadn't really thought that lunch would take her mind off her own problems, but it definitely had. Suddenly, having a husband who cheated, divorce papers that were just recently signed, and looking at her life with no job, no money, bills that were months behind, and the fact that she was back living with her mother didn't seem nearly so bad as the idea of having to police her mother's and her mother's boyfriend's phones for naked pictures.

She had thought she had sunk low, but she hadn't realized how low she could go.

"This is really cute, and it's trending," Grace said as she pointed to an adorable candleholder she found on TakTik, the popular video app that sold a little bit of everything.

"Oh my goodness, that's really cute. And it doesn't look like it would be hard to make at all," her mother said, taking Grace's phone from her and watching the video.

"No. I think we can easily make some modifications to it so our flowers would be slightly fuller and the holder would be more sturdy."

"That would be good. There is a dearth of flowers. And this wouldn't be too expensive to ship either. I do try to take that into consideration, so I'm not ending up charging an exorbitant amount to ship my things."

"All right. I'll try to keep that in mind." Those were the kinds of things that Grace didn't really know about, since she hadn't been helping for a while, but that her mother really had a handle on.

Not only was her mother very positive and always trying to do the right thing, but she was a great businesswoman as well.

"It seems you and Don really seem like you like each other," Grace said, trying to sound casual as her mom handed the phone back. Grace made sure to save that video to her favorites.

She got her notes out and wrote down candleholder under her list of possibilities.

"We just really hit it off. I know that you don't seem to approve, but—"

"It's not that I don't approve. It's just weird. And not in a bad way, just in a way that I need to get used to."

"Weird isn't a good word," her mom said, looking out over her reading glasses at Grace, the way she always had when Grace was little and in big trouble.

"By weird I mean that I'm not used to my mom having a boyfriend. That in itself is a weird sentence to say, and then to see the googly eyes and the secret smiles and the nicknames and…"

Her mom looked concerned and maybe a little hurt.

Grace blew out a breath. "Mom, I am so happy for you, I am over-the-moon ecstatic. I've wanted you to find someone who deserves you and who you deserve, for years, a decade even. But I guess… I guess I never thought about how that would make me feel. Or how that would look, or how I would have to just get used to things, you know?"

"Your life has changed so much. I can understand how this would be a really hard change to accept."

Was that really the problem? Had she just had too many changes in her life in too short of a time?

"I guess maybe you're right in a way. I came back here because it's a safe place to land, and all of a sudden, it's not what I thought it was anymore."

"No, and that's probably my fault. I suppose that Donnie and I could have waited a little longer before we sprung it on you, but… I'm sorry."

"It's fine. I am really happy for you."

"Donnie said Trevor was having the same problem. I actually volunteered you to go talk to him, because I thought you were handling it really well. Maybe I should call him and tell him that you can't do it after all."

She reached for her phone, but Grace stopped her. Was Trevor really having issues? That made her want to help him any way she could. He was such a great guy.

"No. I can talk to him, Mom. If he's really struggling?"

"That's what Donnie says. And Donnie is really worried about him. Did you know that Trevor was actually moving back and moving in with his dad?"

"I guess I did, but in the excitement of...other things...I forgot. Did he get divorced?" She didn't even ask if he had been married. She just assumed that he had, but... That was kind of arrogant on her part. After all, the last she heard, he was in love with her and always would be. That was what he said just before she left.

"No. He never married. He had a good job too. He just didn't like seeing his dad living by himself as he grew older, so he surprised his dad by quitting his job and saying that he was going to start his woodworking business. You know he was always giving you little gifts that he had made."

"I remember that. And then I would put some little decoration on them, to make them more cutesy and feminine, and..." Her eyes drifted to the wall, where her mom still had one of those things hanging. It was a board that he cut a heart into, and she added a bow at the bottom, and a tie at the top, and it just looked rustic and cute and like something that someone online might pay twenty dollars for, and it had cost them nothing, since he had taken the boards from the shed when it was torn down.

"I always thought the two of you made a really good pair. You know how some people just seem to fit together? And complement each other. You aren't opposites exactly, but you just...fit."

Maybe that was what was wrong with her mom and Donnie. She didn't see how they fit. Or maybe, she was so used to seeing her mom fit with her dad and then used to seeing her mom fit in their family, it was unsettling to see her mom fitting with someone else, being with someone else's dad and someone else's family.

Maybe her mom was right. She'd been through a lot of changes, and her mom was just throwing one more at her, which was one too many.

"I really liked him. More than anyone else. And honestly, Lonnie didn't hold a candle to him, although I pretended for a really long time that he did."

"Then why did you leave? I heard he was heartbroken for a long time. I don't know if he ever did get over it."

"I don't know whether he got over it or not, but I do know that Claire always thought I stole him from her. She wouldn't talk to me until I broke up with him, and then I couldn't stay. For that, and other reasons."

Her mom knew about the tragedy that had occurred. She knew how it had shaken all of them and how it made it hard to stay in Raspberry Ridge.

"Sometimes we just have to let the past be in the past. You know?"

Grace wanted to shut that off. After all, her mom hadn't watched one of her friends die. To have her be there one second and completely gone the next, but then... She lost her husband, which had probably been worse. They'd made a family and a home together, had children and a life, plans and love between them. Then one day, it was gone. Just like that.

Ten

"I remember when you were a kid. You loved doing stuff like that." Don looked at the piece of wood Trevor had been working on for the last hour. He'd made it into a decorative birdhouse. Not one that an actual bird would use. At least he hadn't been thinking along those lines, but he supposed it could. But one that could be decorated with little wisps of fabric, some twine or whatever it was called, and hung up either inside or outside of the house.

"I've always loved doing stuff like this. I can't remember a time when ideas weren't coming together in my head." He got a business degree in college and a good job in the suburbs of Chicago. He hadn't hated his work, but it didn't fill his soul and give him total peace the way this kind of work did.

Trevor held the birdhouse up. "If I'm not careful, I'll fill up your garage with all kinds of knickknacks and stuff I make."

"Don't let that happen. Give it away as fast as you make it."

"People will see me coming down the street and start running in the other direction."

"I wouldn't worry about that. Who wouldn't want to have something cute and decorative to hang in their house? Maybe not fifteen of them, but one would be welcome, I'm sure. Or they could give it away as a Christmas gift."

That was true. Maybe people really would appreciate being given the stuff that he made. He enjoyed making it, but that was as far as it went for him. He couldn't imagine what to do with it and didn't have any desire to try to figure out where he could put it in his house, or since he was living with his dad, he wouldn't even consider trying to find a place to hang it in here.

"You know, it's Mrs. Donegan's birthday tomorrow. She might really appreciate someone remembering. I bet it's been years since she got a gift."

Trevor stilled for a moment, his hands freezing. Mrs. Donegan was Claire's grandmother. Claire, the girl who had accused Grace of stealing Trevor from her.

He and Claire had dated once or twice, but he'd never felt anything for her and hadn't wanted to lead her on. She did ask him out, and he'd said a reluctant yes the first time and then tried to make up an excuse every time after that, but she was not easily dissuaded.

Maybe she fancied herself in love with him, or maybe she knew her friend liked him and was trying to stake a claim.

Trevor didn't really know how the female mind worked, but he did know that he'd never been overly interested in Claire, so for her to say that Grace had stolen him was an absolute exaggeration.

"Are you upset about me seeing Gita?" his father said, lifting the mug of coffee that had been sitting on the workbench beside him, and had probably long grown cold, and taking a small sip. It looked perfunctory, since the coffee had to have been ice cold and gross.

So his dad was trying to be casual. Interesting.

Trevor continued to rub the fine-grained sandpaper along the edge of the birdhouse. He didn't want to give an off-the-cuff remark. He actually did have some reservations, but they didn't concern the fact that his dad was seeing a woman. It had more to do with the fact that it just didn't feel quite right.

He'd wanted to be able to talk to Grace about it, but he'd left without getting a moment alone with her, and he hadn't heard from her yesterday at all or at all this morning yet.

She was taking care of her mother, who had just had hip replacement surgery, even though she seemed to be doing really well.

He didn't want to bother her, and maybe he had misread her expressions. But he had gotten the impression that she had just as many reservations as he did, if not more.

"I'm happy for you. I truly am. And I think Mrs. Honea is a really wonderful woman. If you two end up together, it will make me very happy."

"But?" his dad prompted, as though he knew there was more to the story. His dad seemed like he was a little bit hazy and bubbly, but sometimes he could be very astute. This would seem to be one of those times, since Trevor had a hard time hiding the fact that there were issues on his mind.

"It just seems like there's something off. Not in a bad way, necessarily, and not in a way that I don't want you two to be together."

"You think there's a problem with Gita Baby?" his dad asked.

Trevor tried not to flinch. What a nickname. If he called Grace "Gracie Baby," would she slap him across the face as hard as she could or just really, really want to?

Anyway, Gita had more patience than any other woman he knew, but that really wasn't any of his business.

Except... Maybe that was part of the problem. No woman in their right mind would put up with a nickname like that.

Of course, a woman in love wasn't necessarily in her right mind.

"No. I think Mrs. Honea is a superb woman. I think that the two of you will be very happy together."

"Then what's the problem?"

"I'm not sure. It just feels a little off. Like there's something that isn't quite right. And I can't explain exactly what it is." And he was probably just going to make his dad upset and concerned if he continued along these lines. He wasn't trying to break them up.

"So you want us to stop seeing each other?" His dad seemed to be grasping at straws, truly trying to find out what the problem was.

"No. Not at all. I think that the two of you will be very good for each other. And since I can't really put a finger on what the issue is, I hate to even say anything. I don't want you to get the idea that I'm against it. Because I'm not. I could possibly be your biggest cheerleader, although I think Grace would give me a run for my money there." An idea occurred to him, one that he hadn't thought about before. "Do my siblings know about this?" he asked, wondering if he had been the last to know, even though he was the one who was here.

"No. I hadn't told anyone. We… It was like we said last night. We didn't want to tell people until we knew for sure that we were moving ahead."

There was just something in his dad's answer that felt a little…not right. But he couldn't figure out what it was. He didn't want to say he thought his dad was lying, because that wasn't true.

"Are you upset?" his dad asked again.

He knew he shouldn't have said anything. Now his dad was afraid that he wasn't all on board. And that wasn't it at all.

"Maybe it's just the idea of seeing you with someone other than my mom. It just feels…weird." He really didn't think that was what the problem was, but it was the only thing he could think of that his dad would accept, since he couldn't really say for sure what the issue was, and being vague and unhelpful just upset his dad. "I think I'll get used to it eventually."

"Maybe you need to see us together some more. How about we invite them over tonight?"

"Is she able to come this far already?"

"Oh. I forgot about her hip. Maybe we can see if we can go over. We'll make a meal and take it to them. Yeah. People do that when people are sick."

"All right." It seemed like his dad was desperate to be able to go see Gita.

"You know you don't need to have me along in order for you to go visit, right?"

"We told you last night, we want to make sure that we do everything aboveboard. We want to set a good example. So we need a chaperone."

Trevor nodded his head and blew the fine sawdust off the birdhouse, lifting it up and holding it away so he could look at it. It was almost perfect.

"All right. You set it up, and we'll figure out something to cook. Let me know if I need to make a trip to the grocery store."

"Do you have more of that cauliflower? It was really good."

Trevor grinned. "If we're having that, we probably ought to get started. It cooks in the crockpot. And I don't have any, so I will need to make a trip to town."

"Someone should really start a grocery store here."

"I hardly think they'd make enough money to make it worthwhile. The days of a mom-and-pop grocery store being able to support a family are long gone, if they ever existed at all."

"I think they did. Used to be that people went to town once a month and then got whatever they couldn't get at the little store in their hometown. Now, it's nothing to jump in the car and drive to the big box store every day, or every other day, definitely once a week."

Trevor nodded. He knew that to be true. People didn't frequent the mom-and-pop stores like they did the bigger grocery stores. There wasn't as much variety, for one, and the prices were higher for another, and it was cheaper to drive to town to get cheaper groceries than it was to walk to the store and pay twice as much.

They talked a bit about what they could make, and then Don said that he probably ought to call and see if it suited the ladies to have them bring a meal anyway. After all, there was no point in going through the work if they had other plans for dinner.

While he did that, Trevor cleaned up his workspace, using a brush to brush off the sawdust into a container and setting the birdhouse on the work shelf, admiring it a little.

He loved putting it together, but there was something about looking at something that he had made and admiring it that made his heart happy.

Whatever it was with his dad and Mrs. Honea would work itself out. Maybe he was just imagining things. But it wouldn't hurt to talk to Grace. Maybe they could get some time alone this evening, if they ended up having dinner together.

Eleven

"This is absolutely adorable," Grace said as she held up the little craft item she had made from an idea she got on social media. She added a few of her own touches, and it had turned out better than she had anticipated.

"I can't believe how creative you are. I am really good at making something from a pattern, but you're really good at seeing the pattern and then creating something different and unique, and, I might add, better."

"You're my mom, so your opinion might be a little bit biased," Grace said as she smiled lovingly at her mother.

They hadn't talked any more about her mother's new boyfriend or why it had been such a shock to find out about it. How long had her mom been thinking about this? And not telling anyone?

She had sent a quick text to both of her sisters asking if her mom seemed to have any romantic interest, and they both texted back in the negative. Of course, both of them wondered why, and Grace had been hard-pressed to come up with a legit and truthful answer, one that did not incite any more questions.

"Who could I give this to?" she asked, to herself really, but her mom heard and answered right away.

"Mrs. Donegan's birthday is tomorrow. I think we all know that because her husband died on her birthday five years ago. The whole town went out of their way the next year on the one-year anniversary of his death to try to make it a special day for her. Every year since, I've just remembered. I'm sure a lot of other people do too, because I think it's a hard day."

"That would be a really hard birthday for the rest of your life. To have someone you love die on it." She couldn't even imagine. And Mrs. Donegan had gone through some difficult things. Not the least had been what had happened with Claire and everyone.

She didn't want to think about those kinds of sad things today though, so she pushed it aside.

"Do you think she would like this?" she asked, twisting it around and wondering what someone who wasn't related to her would think.

"I think just the idea that you thought of her and took her something would make her feel good. It's too bad that Lauren's mom has been having health problems and has closed the bakery. I know that Mrs. Donegan always had a soft spot for her warm cheese bread."

"I can't imagine anyone not having a soft spot for her warm cheese bread." Grace could feel herself longing for that relic of her past. She could practically smell it now. "Lauren used to talk about taking over someday."

"I remember you guys sitting out on our front porch, talking about how she was going to make bread and other bakery goods, and you were going to make crafts, and you guys were going to stay here and be happy by the lake forever."

"Those were girlhood dreams. Then we grew up and realized that they weren't going to pay any bills. No one's going to get rich operating a bakery in a dinky little town like this, and crafts are not exactly something that are super popular anymore. People want things that are a little bit more sophisticated, and the stuff that I make isn't like that at all."

"Don't sell yourself short. Your stuff looks just as good as anything you could buy in the store. And craft stores are very popular."

Grace didn't argue with her mother. She knew that as much as she loved what she was doing now, there was no way she was going to make enough to support herself. She did hope she could make a living at it at least long enough to be with her mom and take care of her. But she supposed that she probably ought to be looking for an actual job.

"You know, if we had the tourist traffic that some of the towns south of us have, you wouldn't have a problem selling crafts, and Lauren wouldn't have a problem coming back home and taking over her family bakery."

"I haven't talked to Lauren in years. I have no idea if she'd still even want to do that." It was true, she hadn't talked to Lauren for a really long time. Maybe that was the way it always went where people graduated and went to college and barely saw each other anymore. Or maybe it was because of the tragedy that they all went through. It seemed to bind them closer before it blew them all apart.

They didn't say anything else before Gita's phone rang, and she picked it up from where it sat beside her recliner. Grace, who normally worked in the craft room upstairs when she used to help her mom, had brought things to the table so she could sit in the same room as her mom, and her mom didn't have to climb the stairs. They were working on stairs in physical therapy, and her mom was progressing rapidly. She wasn't quite where she was before her surgery, but she was probably at seventy-five percent, at least by the physical therapist's estimation.

"Hello?"

Her mom sat and listened for a little bit, and then a big smile appeared on her face. "I'd love to. That would be wonderful. No, I know that Grace would be on board with that too. Would you like us to make dessert?"

There were a few more minutes of typical conversation, and then Gita hung up.

"I hope it's okay if Donnie and Trevor come over for dinner tonight? I told him we'd make dessert." She gave an apologetic smile. "That basically means you'll be making dessert. Although, I'm allowed to stand up for thirty minutes at a time, and I'm pretty sure I can have a dessert whipped up in that amount of time."

"I can make something." Grace tried to keep her voice even. She hadn't gotten a chance to say anything to Trevor. Now she wished she would have called last night after she went to her room. The thing was, her mom had always had really great hearing. No matter how low she kept her voice, it seemed like her mom could always hear when she was on the phone when she wasn't supposed to be.

Of course, now that she was an adult, she could talk on the phone whenever she wanted to. She just didn't want to bring any attention to herself or have her mom know that she was talking to Trevor, trying to figure out what was going on with her mom and Don.

"That would be wonderful. Will you be able to deliver your craft and still get that done?"

Grace looked at the clock. It was still well before noon. "Sure. I'll have plenty of time. Even if I have to go to the store and grab some ingredients."

"I have really been having a hankering for chocolate cake. I wonder how Donnie feels about cake?" Before she could answer, her mom picked up her phone and started texting.

It wasn't even a minute later before she looked up with a big smile. "Donnie loves chocolate cake."

"I can make a Texas sheet cake then," she said.

"If you do that, you have to go get cocoa. I recall using the last of it the last time I made brownies." Her mother sighed. "That was my little treat before I went to the hospital to have my hip done."

"That's a pretty good treat," Grace said, laughing. She loved that her mom did little things like that. Even for herself. That she was always looking for things that made her smile, and if she couldn't find them, she created them. Getting her hip replaced probably made her very nervous, but instead of focusing on how upset and anxious she was, she made herself brownies and considered that a happy thing.

"I should have time to run this to Mrs. Donegan, and then I'll stop back in and check on you before I run to the store and grab cocoa. Is there anything else we need?" She hated to make such a long trip for just one item, but if they were going to have chocolate cake tonight, she didn't have a choice.

"I'll try to think of anything before you get back. I promise I won't get out of my chair," her mom added, since she knew that it was Grace's job to be watching her.

"Thanks for doing that for me. It definitely eases my mind when I'm not here."

"I know. It's not my job to make your life harder. I'm trying to make it easier, and happy too."

Grace blinked as she walked out of the room, taking the craft with her. It was her job to make it easier, and happy too? There seemed to be something in her mom's words that just didn't quite add up. Not in a bad way, just...like her mom had a subliminal message. Which was ridiculous. Her mom had no guile at all, and she certainly wasn't trying to do subliminal messaging.

Grace changed out of her ratty old T-shirt and put a happy spring top on, pairing it with a pair of capris and flip-flops. She looked suitably presentable to visit Mrs. Donegan and also go to the grocery store. But she didn't look so dressy that she would make anyone feel uncomfortable.

It was a beautiful day to walk, and Mrs. Donegan lived on a small farm, in a huge old farmhouse just a quarter mile off Main Street in Raspberry Ridge. Since it was so nice, and since her mom was doing so well, Grace figured that she could walk.

Plus, she wanted a little bit of time to process, since Mrs. Donegan was Claire's grandmother, and every time Grace thought about Claire, she felt guilty, although she wasn't sure why. It wasn't like she and Trevor were in any kind of relationship now. It was just the idea that she had been accused of something that she didn't feel like she deserved to have the guilt pinned on her for.

If she had done something, she could admit it, apologize, get past it.

But to be accused of something she didn't do, and to feel like people didn't believe her when she proclaimed her innocence, made her just want to accept the fact that everyone was going to believe that she had done it, no matter what she said.

That didn't sit very well with her either.

She passed the farm where Becky and Rodney had recently settled.

Becky was out in the corral working with her horses, the twins she and Rodney had adopted after her sister passed away in a double stroller nearby, and Grace waved as she walked by.

Becky waved back and then put a protective hand on her stomach, almost as though... Wouldn't that be sweet? Their town could use new babies and the joy and life they brought. Particularly at church. Grace hadn't been there for very long and had only managed to go to one midweek service, but babies at church always made everything more interesting and encouraged the current parishioners that there would be a next generation following in their footsteps.

She was old enough now to look back at babies and see that next generation.

It was an odd feeling and an even odder thought. She was deep in contemplation when she realized that someone was calling her name.

She could see the farmhouse up ahead, but the man's voice came from behind her.

She turned and saw Trevor walking behind her.

She laughed a little and tilted her head.

"Are you following me?" she asked, because she couldn't imagine why he would be on this lane. The only place it led was to Mrs. Donegan's old farmhouse.

"It looks like I am, doesn't it?" Trevor said, and then she realized that he was carrying something too.

It looked like a birdhouse, maybe something that he had made himself. She remembered that about him from years ago. He was always whittling on a piece of wood or putting something together. He was even a good artist, which surprised her, since he didn't look like he would be.

"You must be thinking about Mrs. Donegan's birthday as well." She hadn't thought that the entire town knew when her birthday was. That would include Trevor, of course.

"Honestly, I totally forgot about it, although I remember what a tragedy she had on her birthday five years ago."

"Yeah," she said, not saying any more. It wasn't the only tragedy that had happened in Raspberry Ridge over the years, nor the only tragedy that Mrs. Donegan had had to deal with.

"But my dad remembered, and after I made this today, he suggested I take it and give it to her. I know it would mean more if I had made it with her in mind to begin with, but...that's not the way it happened."

"Same for me. I was just making something that I had seen on social media, well, I altered it, gave it a few upgrades, and came up with this." She held up the egg-gathering apron she had made.

"That's really neat." He laughed. "It is perfect for Mrs. Donegan. From what I understand, she rented out her farm years ago, but she still has a bunch of chickens. In fact, my dad told me that while I was out here that if she had any extra eggs, I should grab some."

"I was first, so if she has any eggs, I get first dibs."

"If I get there first, you don't," Trevor said, and then he made as though he were going to start running.

Grace squealed and grabbed a hold of his arm. "No. That's not fair. I waited for you."

"Fine. If she has eggs, we'll split them."

"That's still not fair, but it's better."

"If she has an odd number for sale, you get the extra one."

"All right. Deal." She nodded her head, as though she were satisfied. When in reality, she would like to have farm-fresh eggs, but she could buy them at the store just as easily as she could buy them from Mrs. Donegan. And she hadn't really been intending to purchase them there anyway.

But Trevor didn't need to know that.

"I'm glad to see you. Because I wanted to talk to you." He paused, shook his head, then blurted out, "Wow. Our parents."

She laughed. "That's my feeling exactly. Did your dad say anything to you this morning?"

"Yes, actually he did. I was tempted to call you last night. Because I hadn't heard anything from him then. And still now... I told him it just doesn't feel right to me. There's something...off."

"Something like the fact that my mom isn't getting absolutely and completely annoyed by the fact that he's calling her Gita Baby?" Grace was partially joking, but it was true. It was such a ridiculous nickname.

"Yes. Not exactly. It just makes it feel...fake. Like they're not really together. Because the only thing I can figure was that a woman would only allow herself to be called a name if her mind was addled by being in love. But are they really that much in love?"

"That was what I was wondering about too. But then, my mom's allowed to be in love. It just seems weird. Just because I've known her all my life and she's never acted like that, that doesn't mean she's incapable of it. That doesn't mean she's not allowed either. So maybe the thing that makes me uncomfortable is not the fact that the relationship feels wrong, or fake, but that it just feels weird to see my mom with anyone except for my dad."

"That's the conclusion I came to too. I want to say that there's something off about the relationship, but I think the more accurate thing is that there's something off with the way I'm accepting it. Because it's just weird to see my dad with anyone except my mom. Not that I don't love your mom, and not that I don't think that they're perfect together, and they're two great people who deserve each other. It's just... not what I was expecting."

"I think that's exactly what the problem was with me too. But I feel better having talked to you about it."

Twelve

Grace and Trevor were silent for a bit as they walked along side by side. Grace remembered how perfect Trevor had always felt beside her. It wasn't that they were the same size, since he was a good bit bigger than she was, but it just felt good to have him beside her. Good and right in the kind of way that made peace settle down into her soul and made the world feel happy and bright.

"We spent a good bit of time out here at the farm growing up," Trevor finally said.

"We did. So many happy memories." And everything was ruined by one really, really bad one. Maybe not ruined, since it didn't exactly happen on the farm, but it was a memory that shadows clung to with grippy fingers that sent shivers, and not the good kind, down her spine.

"Too bad about the tragedy."

"Yeah. That's what I was just thinking."

They didn't need to say anything. They both knew what it was. Although Trevor hadn't been there, he'd still been affected, because everyone in their small town had been affected. And Yolanda had been part of the group. Until she was gone. And wasn't anymore. She had more than once come out here to hang out and to have fun on the farm. Where the wide-open spaces beckoned, and there were never-ending things to do and explore. Not like there wasn't a huge lake down below to explore and have fun too. And there were several vantage points on the farm where the views of the lake were just absolutely outstanding.

"It's too bad about that. I think that's why Claire never came back. And this is such a beautiful place."

"Yeah. It's funny how we allow the things in the past to control us." Even as she said that, it made her angry, just a little. After all, she didn't want some random incident from years ago to define who she was today. Although, somehow it did. Not just the tragedy from her youth, but her husband's betrayal, her divorce, the loss of her job, all of those things had beaten her down and made her feel less than.

"Whatever happens to us, our worth is supposed to be because we're a child of God. The creator of the universe, the living God, the master of everything, loves us and considers us His children when we trust in Christ. We're brothers with Jesus."

"And sisters," she said easily, but she knew what he meant. That should trump everything. It should make everything look small in comparison. And it should keep them from allowing themselves to be beaten down by life. But somehow... Somehow she allowed it to happen anyway.

"It's funny how easily we forget. How easily we're swayed by whatever is right in front of us."

"Or whatever looms large in our minds. Why can't God be just as large as tragedy and sadness and regret?"

"And as big as betrayal and mistakes and all the negative things. We make those negative things so much bigger than any positives we could possibly find."

"Not only the positive of God loving us, of being a child of God, finding my worth in Christ, but there's also the positive of how our trials and the things that we've gone through make us better people."

They stopped at the gate to the yard and faced each other automatically, and saw each other trying to grapple with the question and come up with a satisfactory answer.

"I think that's the point of life," Grace finally said.

"What?" Trevor asked, as though he had lost the thread of their conversation. Maybe he had. His thoughts surely weren't going in the same direction that hers were.

"I know that after we're saved, God leaves us here and doesn't take us to heaven right away, because He wants us to tell other people about Him."

"I agree. But I don't see how that fits with what we were talking about."

"I just didn't want you to think I was developing a new reason for us to be here, contrary to what the Bible says."

"Okay."

"But I do believe that as we're left here, we go through these trials, these hard things, and the point of our life is to bring glory to God through them. And that makes us better people, because you can't go through trials without being changed. Sometimes it's for the worse."

"Like when we focus on the bad."

"Exactly. We fail to see God's hand when we insist on looking at how dark and dim things are rather than seeing how God is trying to work in us and change us to be more like Him."

"It's a really hard thing to think about sometimes. Especially when you're grieving, or your heart is broken, or you feel so terrible you just don't have words."

"And like you can't go on." She knew that only too well. She certainly had days—and, if she were being honest, weeks—like that after she found out her husband was cheating on her. She didn't want to go into all of that right now with Trevor.

"But you're saying that focusing on the good makes you better."

"I think so. And I also think sacrifice, when God says to us, do you love me more than this? And whatever it is that He's allowed to be taken from you or whatever hard thing He's asked you to go through or do, you have to be willing to pry your hands up away from what you want and let it go." She had had to learn that about her husband and her marriage and all the dreams that she had for her life.

"You're talking like you have experience."

She looked at the ground, at the sand and stone that were as much a part of her childhood as the wind and the water and the lake itself. "When I got married, I thought I would be married forever." She hadn't been going to talk to Trevor about it, but it seemed like he was interested. And it showed an example of what she was talking about.

"I think we all think that when we get married, don't we?"

"Maybe. I suppose in modern day, there are a lot of people who are thinking, we'll try this and see if it works. But anyway, I thought I would have a fiftieth wedding anniversary. I thought I would have a family, children, grandchildren, you know?" She had been driven to be successful, yes, but she had expected to have all of that as well.

"And?" he prompted her.

"And my husband cheated. He left me. It was pretty bad." That didn't seem like it explained nearly how bad it was. Not even close. "And I was devastated. All of these things that I wanted, that I expected to have, had now been ripped away from me. I wondered why God was doing this to me. Why was He putting me through this trial? Why allow this pain? Why me? Why not someone else?"

"I think those are questions everybody has asked at some point or another. But the question probably should be, why not me?"

"Exactly. But beyond that, I got to thinking, maybe God was saying that I made my marriage my idol. I made the dreams that I had for my life—my family, my kids—idols as well."

"You expect God to give you all good things and no bad." He paused for a moment. "And you can't be saying that it was God's will for your husband to commit adultery?"

"I struggled with that. Why did God do that? It couldn't possibly be His will, right?"

"God's will couldn't include sin, right?"

She shrugged. She really didn't know. After all, David had committed adultery with Bathsheba. It was in the Bible. God didn't approve, but He allowed it to happen. He showed the consequences, and then He used it to bring a blessing to all of Israel, a new king, the wisest man who ever lived.

"I guess I would say that maybe it's not God's will, but He allows it, because He knows that these trials will make me a stronger, better person. But He also wants to know, kind of like Abraham and Isaac, whether I will turn to Him and cling to Him no matter what happens in my life. Is He really the most important thing in my life? Am I really trusting Him? Even when it seems like He's doing me hurt rather than good? That's probably the hardest time in my life that I had to trust God. It just didn't seem like I could turn to Him and depend on Him, because He let me down so much."

"He has never let you down."

While a part of her wanted to argue that Trevor didn't know all the details of her life, his statement was made with complete confidence because he knew the character of God. That made the difference, and that allowed his faith—to know, and believe, to have faith, that God was good and loving and kind and long-suffering all the time. Always.

So, rather than argue, like her old self might have, she had to agree. "That's right. And I think that's what we learn through those kinds of things."

She fingered the top of the fence, picking off a chip of paint. "God, no matter what happens, is always there and never lets us down, no matter how bad it looks. It hurts, it hurts a lot, sometimes we have to go through the pain in order to come out on the other side to the blessings that way. To become the person that He wants us to become. To become more like Jesus."

"And I think learning that made whatever suffering you had worthwhile, even though it probably didn't seem that way at the time."

"Yes. Exactly. I probably would have punched someone in the nose if they tried to tell me that the things I learned from my suffering were going to be worthwhile." She wasn't typically prone to violence, but she could see herself having a violent reaction.

"And why? When someone's just trying to point out something that's helpful, why do we have such a violent, physical, anger-induced reaction?"

"That's a good question, isn't it? Maybe it's jealousy because those people aren't going through the suffering that I am. Or maybe it's the idea that they're trying to tell me that this pain is going to bring something good, something that is hard for me to see. I don't know."

They were quiet for a bit, and she didn't know about him, but her thoughts had gone to Claire, and the tragedy that they had all been involved in, and the tragedy of Mrs. Donegan, having her husband pass away on her birthday. She stroked the egg apron in her hand and then looked back toward the house with its wide, welcoming porch, the planters that would soon be holding beautiful, blooming flowers all summer long, and the rocking chairs that were now empty but would soon have at least one person sitting on them, enjoying the breeze from the lake and the beautiful country air all around.

"I wish Claire would come back," she said softly. Knowing even as she said it that most people didn't go back. Most people lived their lives and, at best, visited the town of their childhood once in a while. More than likely, Claire wouldn't come back until her grandmother passed away and she needed to clean up the house in order to sell it.

"I want to say we can't go backward, but sometimes I feel like I just did. I gave up a good job, moved out of the suburbs, and came back to my dad. Why? It feels like I'm going backward."

"You're not as backward as I am. I didn't give up a good job, I got fired." She hadn't meant to say that either. But she always felt comfortable with Trevor, and words slipped out. Even after they hung in the air, she didn't regret them. It was the truth. She'd been fired.

"I'm sorry to hear that. It must have been terrible on top of your husband cheating."

"Yeah. I was really good at my job, but when he left, it was a struggle to get out of bed, and every day, I got more and more behind. I wasn't able to do the things that I needed to do, but I managed to stay afloat. But when I knew for sure that I would be getting divorce papers, and we talked about splitting our assets, I just lost it. I didn't get out of bed for three days. Employers have a problem with stuff like that."

"I see. I'm sorry."

"I guess it's kind of like everything we've been talking about. I don't know if there was a reason for me to come back here, but it really was my only choice. Maybe God will work everything out for good."

"He promises to. That's a promise I've clung to more than once. Although never to the degree that you have to right now."

"I guess it was terrible at the time, but once I made the decision that I was going to have to move back, and I had to start cleaning out my condo, I kind of...accepted it." That was mostly true. She supposed she still had days where she wondered why she was going backward rather than forward. "It was a humbling thing, you know? And I needed that."

"I suppose we all can use a little bit of humbling at times."

He hadn't given her a hard time for leaving without properly breaking up with him or even talking to him at all. Maybe he wasn't thinking about that anymore. She'd already apologized for it, and he certainly hadn't asked her to.

"When I left, I was arrogant. I thought I had the world by the horns. I thought I was going to be so successful by the world's standards." She paused for a moment, knowing that they needed to go in. If Mrs. Donegan was looking out the window, she had to be wondering what in the world they were doing.

She shook her head. "I thought leaving made me better. You know? I wasn't one of those losers who stayed in this tiny hometown. I was making something of myself in the city, because everyone knows the city's all that." There was sarcasm in her voice, because she didn't believe that now. In fact, if anything, her excursion into the city had taught her that it was worse. Much worse.

"That's where some good has come," he said, and she nodded.

Time for a subject change. "Mrs. Donegan's probably wondering what in the world is going on. We better go in."

She didn't really want to move. She could stand and talk to Trevor all day. Just like they'd never left each other, like he was still her best friend.

He grinned, and even that reminded her of the time they spent together. So much of it had been spent laughing. She loved that grin. Loved tracing his lips with her finger, kissing them with her own.

She couldn't think like that. Instead, she unlatched the gate. He pushed it open and allowed her to go through first. She didn't wait for him, but they walked single file up the walk and onto the front porch. She glanced at him as she lifted her hand and knocked on the door.

His eyes were thoughtful, almost as though he were remembering too. Did he feel it? Feel the laughter and the pull of the happy memories? The way they seemed to fit together, and how talking to him was easy and enjoyable. Did he feel the same brightness deep down in his soul? The same feeling of just being with the perfect person?

There was no white-hot, burning passion. But rather a simple, easy, friendship-type feeling. The idea that there could be more. That she wanted to be closer to him, that snuggling in his arms would feel like she had come home. Even more than walking into her mother's house and smelling the old, familiar scents that brought her childhood back in full memory.

They didn't say anything as they waited for Mrs. Donegan to open the door. She could hear movement in the house, and though it took a while, she didn't knock again. The older woman probably just moved slowly and needed some time to get to her door.

Eventually, the door cracked open, and Mrs. Donegan, the same yet older, stood in front of them. Same white hair, but maybe a little bit whiter and much thinner. The same smiling blue eyes, although more crinkles and perhaps even more deeply set in the sockets. Same faded housedress, the same friendly smile. But older.

It reminded her that she wasn't a little girl again. She was a woman, and she should be making more mature decisions. Maybe one of those decisions should be to reach out to her friends. Was that the mature thing to do?

"Hello. Mrs. Donegan?"

"That's me. Are you selling something?" the lady asked, not sounding belligerent, exactly, but like she was going to send them packing if they were.

"No. Your birthday is tomorrow, and we made some things for you. But I don't think you remember me. I'm Grace. Grace Honea," she said, supplying her maiden name and not her married name of Tyack. She hadn't considered, but she could go back to using her maiden name. She wouldn't mind losing the name of the man that she had married, who had betrayed her. It wasn't like she had children who would care.

She shook that thought away to consider later. It was the first time she had thought about it, and she didn't want to do anything rash.

"Grace! You and Claire used to be good friends."

"We did. And you probably remember Trevor Gillett too."

"I do indeed. A handsome young man back in the day, and you're still that way. Are you two back in town?"

"We are," Trevor answered while Grace was trying to figure out how to. She supposed his answer was correct. She didn't know for how long. She had just been thinking that morning that she wouldn't be able to make a living making crafts, but...her mother had for years. Maybe if she was careful, maybe if she worked hard, which she didn't mind the thought of at all since she loved crafting. It would be a dream come true to be able to make a living doing something she loved.

But what about when the thing that she loved doing became work instead of fun? Whether it was working or fun, at least she wouldn't have a betraying, cheating scoundrel of a husband stuck to her anymore.

The thought should have made her happy, but it made her sad instead. Still, the things that Trevor and she had just talked about came to her mind, and she determined that she was going to go out of her way to look for the positive things and focus on those.

"I just moved in with my dad, and Grace just moved in with her mom. Apparently, the two of them are seeing each other." Trevor lifted his shoulder as though saying, who knew?

"Oh my goodness. Well, that's news!" Mrs. Donegan said, stepping back from the door as she opened it. "Please come in. I'd love to catch up more. My goodness, Don Gillett and Gita Honea seeing each other. Wow. Who would have thought?" she said, shaking her head as she stood back and waited for them to walk in the house.

Grace hadn't exactly expected to have a long, drawn-out visit, since she still had to go to the grocery store, after she checked on her mom again, but the whole point of their visit was to spend a little time with Mrs. Donegan and make her smile during a time that should be happy but might have been sad. If they ended up spending time sitting around her table talking, that was time well spent.

Thirteen

"Please sit down. Would you like some coffee or tea?" Mrs. Donegan indicated the kitchen table.

It was a little bit chilly outside, but Trevor would have preferred to sit out on that beautiful front porch. Of course, the memories were harder out there than they were in here. They spent precious little time in the farmhouse. Mrs. Donegan had made them treats galore over the summer. They'd usually eat them outside. Sometimes on the porch, but more often, they ran in, grabbed their treats, and then ran back out to the barn loft or even down the steep trail beside the cliff to the lake.

"I'd love some tea, please," Grace said.

"I'd take some coffee, if it's not too much trouble. I already had a cup today, so don't make anything special for me." He typically only drank one cup a day, but for Mrs. Donegan, and to make her smile, he would drink two.

She seemed happy to have people to serve, to visit with, to talk to. And she seemed almost gleeful at the idea of his dad and Grace's mom being together.

"You two were together for a while in high school, weren't you?" she asked as she shuffled around the kitchen. When she was younger, Trevor would have called it bustling, but now...it was more like a slow shuffle.

"We were for a while. Until I ran off. It was a mistake on my part. But enough of that," Grace said, all in one breath, as though she didn't want to have to talk about that any more than she had to.

And he didn't blame her. He didn't really like talking about it either, at least talking about the end, when she left him. He wouldn't mind talking more about how they were together and the memories that they had.

He wondered if she remembered anything. Did she feel the same way he had when they had been talking by the gate? The feeling that it was perfectly right for them to be together? That she was the one for him and always had been? That's what he felt. He always felt that way around her. The idea that Claire would say that she had stolen him made it even more ludicrous, considering that he never felt like he belonged to anyone but Grace.

"Oh. I almost forgot. Here I am holding this. I made this for you," Grace said, pulling out the egg apron she carried and unfolding it on the table.

Mrs. Donegan turned around and put a hand to her chest. "My goodness. That's for me?"

"I'd heard that you sold your cows not long ago, but you still have chickens, and I thought this might be something you could use. I got the idea for it online, so… I guess I don't know if it's practical or not."

A cute little redness brightened her cheeks, and Trevor wanted to run a finger over one of them, to tease her a bit, to bring it out more, or just to make her smile. He resisted all of those urges. That wasn't his right.

It used to be, but it wasn't anymore.

"Oh my goodness. Isn't this nice," Mrs. Donegan said as she lifted the apron and held it up to her front.

"Happy birthday. I know it's a day early, but I just wanted to give you something."

"Wow. I haven't seen you for years, and you remembered my birthday."

It looked like Mrs. Donegan was close to tears. Trevor stepped in.

"And I made you this. It could use a little decoration, but it might be cute for you to hang somewhere. In fact, if you figure out where you want it, I'll hang it for you."

He hadn't been planning on saying that last part, but the idea of Mrs. Donegan with a hammer was kind of ludicrous, although obviously the woman still went out and collected her own eggs, so she must be a lot more capable than what he was giving her credit for.

Still, she put a hand on her chest again, and her eyes really did fill with tears. He hadn't said anything, and tears made him especially uncomfortable.

"My goodness. All of this bounty in one day. This is beautiful. Is it a real birdhouse? Could I put it outside and birds will nest in it?"

"I think so. I don't see why they wouldn't. It would have to be a bird of a certain size and type, obviously," he said, indicating the size of the hole.

"I don't know what I did to deserve this, but I thank you both from the bottom of my heart. You...made a time of year that is sometimes difficult for me special."

"We have a lot of great memories growing up here. Playing with Claire and the rest of our friends here. Of the treats that you made for us, and of the way you made our summers special. It was just something that I wanted to do."

"Same. I guess I wasn't as close to Claire as Grace was, but she said it perfectly. I have great memories here, and it makes me happy to see you smile."

"My Benny died on my birthday five years ago. I was moping around the house this morning thinking about what a terrible birthday it was going to be, and then you two show up. Maybe Benny sent you."

"Well, if he did, I would have been freaked out, so I'm glad that I wasn't aware of it," Grace said, and Trevor held his breath until Mrs. Donegan laughed. He had forgotten what a great sense of humor she had. But it was obvious that Grace had said just the right thing, and instead of crying, Mrs. Donegan was laughing.

Grace was so good at stuff like that. She complemented him beautifully, because he could make small talk, but she could turn the conversation and fit it to the person that they were with.

He loved that about her, the little things she remembered, the way she cared about people.

"Tell me about your parents," Mrs. Donegan said as she poured Grace a cup of tea and then set a mug of coffee in front of him before pulling out a chair and sitting down with her own cup of steaming coffee.

He reached out to put a little cream in his while Grace spoke.

"We were just as surprised as you seem to be. I didn't even know they were talking to each other. But... I've been out of town for a while."

"And I don't get off the farm as much as I should. I barely went to church at all this winter. I was afraid I was going to slip on a patch of ice and fall down and break my hip and then my kids would send me off to a nursing home. I'd love it if someone would come and live with me." She said that last part softly, almost as though she didn't really realize she was saying it out loud.

"I haven't seen Claire in years. Where is she?" Grace asked, not responding to her comment directly but maybe wondering why Claire hadn't come back.

"Oh, she's happily married with kids and enjoying the life that she's living in the city," Mrs. Donegan said, waving her hand in the air as though it didn't matter and wasn't important and as though she hadn't just said she wished someone would come live with her.

"I suppose she comes back to visit," Trevor said, hoping that he was right. Because it could disintegrate into sadness and negativity if she didn't.

"They all do. Periodically. More than I should expect, I suppose. Since I'm just a boring old lady and they have much more interesting lives away from here."

"I don't recall you being boring," Grace said right away.

"I haven't been bored," Trevor added, wishing he had the right words to make her feel better but knowing that this was something that everyone had to go through. Almost everyone. The idea that the kids were gone, the grandkids were gone, and maybe they weren't as relevant as they used to be.

"But your mother has found happiness again. Are they thinking of getting married?" Mrs. Donegan asked, after visibly composing herself.

"I guess we're wondering the same thing. We just found out recently and are adjusting. It's so weird to see my mom with anyone but my dad."

"And it's tough for me to see my dad with anyone but my mom. Grace and I were just talking about how it's been an adjustment for us."

"I think anything like that is an adjustment." She sighed. "Your mom was a lot younger than I was when she lost her husband. Perhaps I would have been interested in trying to find someone."

"It's not too late. I've heard of people your age and older finding someone and being happy."

"I suppose I would have to move somewhere. Because I'm not currently in the path of any older gentlemen who might be interested in getting married again." Mrs. Donegan seemed to have forgotten about her sadness and smiled gently.

"Well, I'm an eligible gentleman, and I somehow stumbled into your kitchen this morning. The coffee is delicious, by the way," Trevor said. A little gentle flirting with an eighty-year-old lady wasn't completely terrible.

She laughed, like she enjoyed it, and Grace smiled as though she appreciated his attempt at being kind as well.

"If you just came in here to flatter me, Trevor, I'm wise to your ways. Remember, I knew you when you were getting your diaper changed."

"I'll keep that in mind," Trevor said, trying to pretend he wasn't embarrassed, but he could feel the tips of his ears warming and figured they were red.

Yeah, after looking in Grace's laughing eyes, he figured they were beet red.

Still, it was hard for him to look away, because the laughter on her face was so compelling to him. It drew him and made him want to get closer. Yet, he wasn't sure they could turn their relationship into a friendship. Were they friends? Or were they just two people who used to date, who were dealing with the fact that their older adult parents were interested in each other?

"You'll have to let me know if anything exciting happens. After all, everyone loves to hear a good love story." Mrs. Donegan smiled, and while Trevor didn't consider himself a great romantic, he supposed it was true that everyone loved to hear a great story with a happy ending, and love stories typically were. At least for a while.

He thought about Grace and what she had been through with her ex-husband. And to his shame, part of him was happy about it. After all, it was because her ex-husband had cheated and left her that she was available.

But she had been through so much. He highly doubted that she would be interested in striking up a relationship with him. How long had she said it had been? A year?

He didn't know how long it took to heal from that type of thing, but as devoted as Grace was, as hard as that betrayal must have been, it would probably take her a while.

He was sure she would be a better person. She was deliberately trying to do that, to take what she had been given, the life that she had in front of her, and to make something beautiful out of it.

He admired that. So many people, when bad things happened, questioned God, shook their fists at Him, and got angry that He would allow something so terrible to happen to them. But she seemed to be seeing that terrible things didn't have to have terrible results. It was a perplexing but truthful thing to say that a lot of times the best things happened out of, or because of, the worst things.

They chatted at the table a bit more, but before he knew it, his coffee cup was empty, and they were standing, with him promising to come and put up the birdhouse wherever Mrs. Donegan decided that she wanted it, and both of them promising to come see her again. Since he was moving into town, he could keep that promise, and he really hoped Grace would do it with him. Because it seemed like everything he did with Grace was better than doing it with anyone else.

Fourteen

"That was fun," Grace said as they pushed open the gate and walked out of the yard.

Trevor turned around, making sure to latch it behind him. "I agree. I wasn't sure what to expect when we got there, but Mrs. Donegan seemed really happy to see us, and I admit, I had a good time. It makes me happy to think that our visit made her happy."

"Isn't that interesting? How making someone else happy makes us happy, happier than we would be if we were just running around trying to make ourselves happy all the time."

"That was a lot of happiness, but I think I followed you," he teased, and she laughed as he figured she would. They had so many good times together, and he was pretty sure she hadn't forgotten any of them. No more than he had.

"I was thinking while we were sitting there," she started.

"You're scaring me," he teased. What was it about Grace that brought out the teasing in him? It was probably just because he wanted to see her smile. Which she did.

"Oh goodness. Stop already."

They started down the lane, and he said, "I'm sorry. What were you thinking?"

"I was thinking that after talking to Mrs. Donegan, she was so happy that our parents were happy, and I thought...we should do everything we can to get them together. You know? I mean, not that I've been trying to keep them apart, because I haven't. But the idea of us doing what we can to help the relationship along. You know?"

He considered it. "Like...you and I will make excuses to be together so that our parents can be together too?"

"Kind of. I don't know. I didn't really think of any specifics, I was just thinking about the general idea of wanting to help them. I want them to be able to have this second chance at love at their age, because it could be twenty or thirty years that they get to spend together. That's longer than my marriage lasted anyway."

"It's longer than a lot of marriages last," he said, hoping that made her feel better. It was true.

She smiled at him, as though she appreciated his effort.

He felt his gaze cut to hers, and the same feeling that had been swirling around ever since they met on the lane took hold inside of him.

He wanted to say something to her. Wanted to suggest that maybe they could be more or see if she wanted to do something with him, just for the sake of being with him.

But before he could say anything, she said, "If we can convince our parents that they need to be together in order to encourage us to be together, I think we'll have it made. They'll spend as much time as they possibly can together, because... I think they both want us to be happy." She lifted her shoulder. "I saw that last night with your dad. I mean, beyond the oddness of seeing him with my mom and hearing him call her Gita Baby, there was...a feeling I got when I watched how he looked at you. It was just the look of someone who wants the very best for their child."

"I haven't been a child for a while." He didn't know why that exact statement came out of his mouth. He understood what she was saying. But... He didn't want her to think of him as a child. It bothered him that she had been looking across the table at them and thinking about him as less than what he was.

"No. I know that." She paused. "Trust me, I know that."

Her reply made him look at her. But she wasn't paying any attention to him. She had her gaze on the ground and one lip pulled in between her teeth, deep in thought.

He wanted to ask what she was thinking about, but maybe he didn't want to know.

"What do you think we could do?"

"I was trying to think of activities we could all do. Your dad seems to be pretty athletic, but my mom... I don't know if she could keep up with him. Especially with her hip. She's really been coming along fast, though."

"We could rent double kayaks. They could be in one, we could be in the other."

"That's a great idea," she said, her eyes shining as she looked up. She met his gaze, and he had to focus in order to continue to think about what they were talking about, instead of being distracted by how he felt about her.

"Grace?" he asked, even though he didn't know what he was going to say.

"Yes?" she said, looking at him with her brows raised, almost as though she were expecting him to add to her suggestion.

"The worst pain in my life was the pain when you left."

Why did he say that? He didn't want to take away from the happy time that they were having. Didn't want to bring her down from the smiles and laughter that they'd been sharing. From the good feeling he had from making Mrs. Donegan smile. But it was the truth. When she'd been talking about her heartbreak and her husband cheating and all the pain in her life, and the lessons that she learned, that had been his worst time.

As he had been afraid of, her face fell. Her shoulders slumped, and he knew he hurt her. He hadn't meant to.

"I'm so sorry. I know it doesn't make anything any better, and I know we talked about how our trials make us stronger and all of that, but can I just say that was the worst mistake of my life?" She lifted her brows and looked at him.

He wasn't sure what she was saying. That walking away from him was the worst mistake of her life? Leaving Raspberry Ridge? Or leaving their friend group? Maybe it was just riding out of town with a feeling of superiority and the desire to make her life successful. She alluded more than once to her arrogance and how dumb she'd been. Even if she didn't use those words exactly.

"That helps," he said. It did too. He couldn't go back and make the pain less. Or make it last a shorter time. It was gratifying to know that if she could do it over, she wouldn't have done it.

"Maybe you don't want to try to spend time with me in order to get our parents together. Maybe you don't want to be with me at all and would prefer our parents don't end up together?"

"No. None of that's true. I would spend time with you, even if it weren't for our parents. But," he hurried to add, lest she think that he wanted something real, which he did, but he didn't want to say right away. "I'm happy trying to get our parents together. I think they'll find a lot of joy and meaning in life if they share it. I do think life is better when shared."

"I agree. Being that I've been alone now for the last year, and I've been trying to separate my life, my life now anyway, from the life I had been building together with someone else, it was nicer when there were two of us. Someone to talk to, share with, get advice from, and do things with."

Those were all the kinds of things he wanted to do with her, but maybe it was a little bit early to talk about it.

"All right then, Dad and I will be coming to your house to eat dinner with you and your mom, and then sometime during the meal, maybe we can suggest that we should go kayaking."

"I think it's important to try to keep them active. It seems like as you get older, you have a tendency to slow down, and people who slow down eventually leave us."

He nodded. "I've been reading literature on that actually. That there is a direct correlation between people who stay active into their senior years, and people who live longer. I suppose I can try to do a little bit more to try to keep my dad active."

"And I'll try to keep my mom active, and hopefully the two of them will get together and keep each other active."

They grinned together, and he felt satisfied. They had a date for tonight, and another day kayaking, if they could get their parents to agree with it.

"Will your mom be able to with her hip still healing?" he asked.

"We might have to plan for next week, but we can see what the physical therapist says. I believe they said she was about seventy-five percent when they came last. So it's not going to be long."

"Good to know. It's nice that her surgery and recovery has been uneventful."

"I know. I can't imagine trying to be in the hospital, trying to make the best decisions possible. I guess that was another thing that made me think I needed to get my mom to be more active. She'll do better with these types of things the more active she is. Not that she wasn't walking already."

"Walking is good, but there's so much more she can do."

Grace nodded, and they continued walking together side by side. He didn't know what she was thinking, but he was thinking about the two of them and being active together as they reached their senior years. Maybe he was just engaging in some wishful thinking, like he had in high school, where he thought they would be together.

There could be children too. They weren't too old for that, and he would like that a lot. Of course, there was no way he'd mention that to Grace, and she hadn't mentioned that or even hinted about it when talking about her husband, other than she had to give up her dreams. And again, he thought that maybe she still needed time to process and heal.

He felt impatient, and he tried to tamp it down and just enjoy the day and the woman who walked beside him. After all, it was the little moments like those that made a life.

Fifteen

"That cake looks really good. And it smells even better." Gita stood beside the counter, looking at the Texas sheet cake that Grace had finished not that long ago.

"Just relax. It won't be long, and we can try it out."

"I remember telling that to you. I also remember making batter just so we could eat it. I feel like I should be reaping what I sowed, but I didn't today."

Her eyes twinkled, and she looked so happy that Grace almost grabbed her in a hug. When was the last time she'd seen her mom this happy?

Well, that was a very good question considering that she hadn't been around a whole lot, so maybe her mom had been this happy, and she just hadn't noticed. But she didn't think so. She was pretty sure the imminent arrival of a certain gentleman was putting that spark in her eyes and that spring in her step even though she wasn't far removed from hip replacement surgery.

"I'm sorry I didn't make a special cake batter just for us to eat together. Maybe next time?" she asked, lifting her brows and giving her mom a baleful look. After all, her mom was an adult and shouldn't expect to get batter every time they made a cake.

"I'll make sure that there's a next time, and I'll remind you of your promise," her mom said, but then she winked and grinned again, and Grace couldn't do anything but smile back. Her mom's face was fresh and cheerful, and the whole atmosphere of the house just seemed to be anticipatory.

If this was how her mother was when she was in love, Don was going to have no choice but to fall so deeply in love with her he couldn't stand to live without her. She was attractive and irresistible and would surely pull him into her orbit.

Even on her worst day, her mother was an attractive woman with a compelling personality, but being in love had ratcheted that up to the next level.

Was that the way every woman wanted? Grace asked herself. Was that the way she was?

She could feel her lips wanting to turn up when she thought about Trevor and their bargain of deciding that they would try to be together in order for their parents to be able to spend as much time as possible together. It felt fun to have a little secret between the two of them, and it also felt good to be doing something so nice for someone else. Even more, it felt good to see her mom so happy. And it wasn't exactly a hardship to be around Trevor. Maybe... Maybe him being around her would make him see that he still loved her after all.

That felt like maybe it was a long shot, but her hopes flew up and made her lips turn into a real smile.

"You look happy," her mother said as she carried silverware from the kitchen into the dining room and placed it around the table.

She was walking without a limp, completely normally. Her physical therapist had been impressed with her progress the day before.

"I'm happy because you're happy. You're practically glowing. You and Don are good for each other."

"I should hope so, because he's a wonderful gentleman," her mom said.

There was a little bit of a feeling of something being not quite right, but Grace pushed it aside as usual. She and Trevor had decided that the feeling stemmed mainly from the fact that they were not used to their parents not being with their other parent. It had nothing to do with any real problem in the relationship.

It was nice to have Trevor to talk things over with so that she could organize her brain and not continually wonder what the problem was. Now that she knew what it was, she ought to be able to put it to rest.

"We should light candles," her mom said.

Grace smiled to herself. Her mom was really going all out.

"Don't you think you should take things a little bit slow?" she said, teasing her mom a bit. After all, that would be something that her mom might have said to her back in the day.

"I am taking things slow. We have chaperones, and we already decided that we're not going to see each other again until next week."

"All right," Grace said and was a little surprised at the disappointment that rumbled through her. If they didn't see each other until next week, she wasn't going to get to see Trevor until next week either.

But that wasn't supposed to matter. And she could use the extra time to really dig into her mother's business and see if there was going to be a spot for her. If there wasn't, she was going to need to find a job.

There was a knock at the door before she could say anything else, and to her surprise, her mother hurried to answer it. Well, she didn't hurry exactly, but she walked gracefully, which Grace had to stop and take a minute to watch. It was amazing how her hip replacement had gone so smoothly, and she was thrilled that her mom was doing such a good job. It didn't hurt to admire that and to be happy for her.

"Hello, Donnie!" she heard her mother say and then watched as Don and Gita embraced.

Don murmured, "Hello, Gita Baby."

Grace met Trevor's eyes, standing slightly behind his dad as their parents embraced, and they shared a smile. It was a laughing, they're using their nicknames kind of smile, but also a we're happy for our parents kind of smile too.

She truly was happy for them.

She could tell by the look on Trevor's face that he was too.

"Trevor, it's good to see you," her mom said with the typical hospitality that she displayed so easily. "Come on in, both of you. That smells delicious," she said, indicating whatever it was that Trevor carried.

"This is more of the cauliflower that we had yesterday, since it was such a big hit," Don said, indicating the small crockpot he held.

"And this is tuna casserole, which, considering that you're dealing with two unmarried men, is no small feat."

"I thought I smelled tuna noodle casserole. I haven't had that in forever, and I can't wait to try it. I hope it has lots of cheese," her mom said, leading them to the table.

"You're not limping," Don observed.

"Nope. The physical therapist told me that I'm doing awesome, although I still need to be very careful not to fall. So, I just take it slow, make sure my steps are measured, and I've been doing pretty well."

"You have. You're back to your graceful self."

"The pain is mostly gone. Every once in a while, I feel a twinge, but I can't believe how well I feel."

"The doctor said it was because she was so active." Grace felt like she could throw that in there, so hopefully later when they suggested they take the double kayaks onto the lake, they would be agreeable.

"That's good news. Whatever the reason," Don said as they sat themselves in chairs at the table.

Don said grace, and then they passed the food around. It did smell really good, even though it was simple, and it tasted even better.

Grace was on her third bite when Trevor cleared his throat, and she looked up to meet his eye.

He lifted a brow, and she nodded ever so slightly. Whatever they were going to do, he was going to get started on now, and that was just fine with her.

"So," he said, getting the attention of both Gita and Don as they chewed. "Grace and I met on the road on the way to Mrs. Donegan's house. We had such a great talk, and you know we have history, and we decided that..."

As he seemed to struggle for words, Grace decided that she could try to help him. "We decided that we would like to develop a relationship together. But we didn't want to interfere with yours and Don's," she said, looking at her mom. "So we were hoping that you two would be our chaperones," she said, lifting a brow at Trevor.

They hadn't exactly talked about that, but it seemed like a good enough excuse for them to try to be together and to get their parents to be together too.

"I don't know if anything will come of it, but that's what we were talking about, and we really wanted to take the kayaks out on the lake together. We hoped that you two might be game to join us?" Trevor said, seeming to be relieved when Grace smiled and nodded.

They were going a little bit off script, but it felt like the right thing to say and do.

"My goodness. I haven't been out on kayaks in years," Gita said.

"Trevor and I go all the time. We can get a double kayak, and you and I could do it together." Don seemed to be all in on the idea.

"Donnie, you have the best ideas. And then Grace and Trevor could have a double kayak, and they could go together as well." Her mother seemed especially pleased about the idea.

"I think that's a fabulous idea," Trevor said.

"I agree. I'd love to go out on the lake with you guys. And I feel like I need to share a kayak with Trevor, because if you guys are used to doing it, I probably couldn't keep up."

That part was one-hundred-percent honest. Loving the idea of going on a boat with Trevor was absolutely true as well. She did want to and did look forward to it. And she wanted the relationship to be real, even though she knew that it really wasn't. At least not in his eyes.

They finished up the meal, talking about different kayak trips they'd taken over the years and a strategy for this one, which included staying close to the shore, just in case anything happened, since neither Grace nor Gita had been out for a very long time. Gita also said that she would check with her physical therapist and perhaps her doctor to make sure that everything was okay and to get the all clear. They agreed that if they didn't get the okay this week, they'd just postpone the trip until they did and substitute something else in. They batted some ideas around, including walking on the beach, taking a drive, or renting mopeds.

Grace didn't even know it was a thing to rent mopeds, but apparently Don and Trevor had done it and had really enjoyed it.

It needed to be a warm day. Of that she was certain.

Regardless, by the time she cut the chocolate cake and finally put a piece in front of Gita, her mother surprised her with her comment.

"I was speaking with Madeline Grosheck earlier today. You know, Lauren's mom?" Gita looked at Grace and waited until she nodded.

She hadn't talked to Lauren in forever, but her mom, Madeline, had operated the bakery until a few years ago when her health took a turn for the worse.

"I haven't seen her in years," Grace said.

"No, she hasn't been well. But she did say when I was speaking with her that Lauren might be coming to pay her a visit. Perhaps even moving back. She wasn't sure."

Grace nodded, and Trevor said something, but she missed it. Because she was thinking that she had just thought she wanted to get in touch with all of her old friends. That would be Lauren and Claire mostly. They were the ones that had run around in their group together along with Yolanda. Until the accident.

"Madeline asked about you. She wanted to know how both of you were doing," she said, looking between Grace and Trevor.

"I should reach out to Lauren," Grace said.

"You should. I hope it's okay that the next time I talk to Madeline, I can tell her that you and Trevor are together."

Fear shot through Grace. She hadn't considered the implications of this. The whole town would know that they were together, and then the whole town would be upset and wondering whose fault it was when they "broke up." It was kind of hard to break up with someone that one wasn't truly with. As she wasn't exactly with Trevor. They were only together, in a fake kind of way, to try to get their parents together. Because they decided that their parents deserved every shot at happiness, which seemed like a kind, considerate reason. But a breakup wasn't going to go over well, and she wasn't sure a fake relationship was something they could admit to the entire town.

"I think Trevor and I would kind of like to keep it between ourselves for a little bit, wouldn't we, honey?" She paused a little before the "honey," stumbling because it was so familiar. She was sure everyone at the table noticed, but hopefully they chalked it up to the fact that the relationship was so new.

"I think Grace is right. This is new, and we're not sure exactly where it's heading. We just want to make sure we do it right. Right, darling?" He did a much better job of calling her darling than she had of using an endearment for him.

Maybe she should call him Trevor Baby. That seemed to roll off Don's tongue like chocolate melted in the sun.

"Gita Baby, not to change the subject or anything, but this is the best chocolate cake I've ever eaten in my life," Don said, and Grace almost laughed when she saw that his mouth was full. Either he was in a hurry to change the subject, or he was truly inspired by the cake.

"I wish I could take credit for it, but Grace made it. I actually complained to her, because this is the cake that my children loved to eat the batter from growing up, and I admit that on more than one occasion, I made the batter just so we could sit and eat it."

"It was always a huge treat. Maybe after we had a really hard test, or for the last day of school, or if something terrible happened. I'm sure that it created lifelong bad eating habits I'm still fighting to this day, but the memories are really sweet." Grace smiled, and Trevor laughed.

"I considered asking her to just serve the batter, but I didn't want you to think we were barbaric."

"It sounds really good, and good trumps being barbaric all day long."

"Good to know." Gita's cheeks had gotten red, and Grace marveled that her mother could still blush at her age.

They talked a bit more, and then the men helped them clear off the table and do the dishes before they sat back down at the table and played a few games.

Grace marveled at how much fun she had with Trevor and his dad. She wouldn't have guessed that they would get along so well, but it had been a long time since she had had that much fun, and she was truly sad when Don and Trevor reluctantly rose and said it was time to go home.

She wasn't able to get a private message to Trevor, but there would be plenty of time for them to talk later. All in all, she thought the evening had been a smashing success.

Sixteen

Gita tiptoed into her bedroom, forgetting about her hip for just a moment, and softly closed the door behind her.

She was pretty sure that Grace was sound asleep. She had retired to her room more than an hour ago, claiming that she had a good time, but she was exhausted.

Gita didn't doubt it, but something was off, and she couldn't wait to talk to Don to try to figure out what it was.

Pulling her phone out from her pocket where she stashed it, she listened quietly for a moment before she sank down in the chair beside her bed and dialed Don's number. She had been sleeping in the chair up until the last few days, when the physical therapist had cleared her to get in and out of bed if she wanted to.

She pulled up his contact info, hit the call button, and waited impatiently for him to answer, tapping her finger on the chair and trying not to give in to the inclination to get up and pace the room.

Don answered on the fourth ring in a small, quiet voice. "Hello?"

"Is he asleep?" Gita asked immediately.

"I think so. That's why I told you it was okay."

"I think Grace is asleep too, but I'm going to keep my voice down just in case."

"Yeah. It seems like that's wise."

"Did you feel like something was off when they started talking about how they were going to have a relationship and they wanted us to chaperone them?"

"It sounded very much like what we had said."

"Do you think they were mimicking us? Did they figure us out?"

"I'm not sure. But why else would they have suggested that we take a kayak trip on the lake? And I think it was Trevor who suggested we sit back down at the table and play games. So, it's not really tracking."

"I agree. Something just feels off. It was very much like what we did, but different, but... They're not...genuine." She wasn't sure if that was the exact word she meant. They did seem to really like each other. She wanted to talk to Don about that before this happened. That she thought that their plan was going well.

"I thought everything was going really great until tonight," Don said, sounding a little disgusted. Still talking softly.

"I agree. I was really thrilled with how things are going. In fact, I almost wanted to talk to you about a victory lap. Because they seemed like they were really getting together."

"But now they're saying they're together, and we don't believe it. Maybe we're the ones who are being weird."

Gita thought about that for a moment. He could be right. Maybe she had gotten so into her role of fake relationship and pretending to have something going on with Don that when they were successful in what they were trying to achieve, she didn't like it, and it didn't feel right.

"I suppose that could have happened. I'll think about that a little bit. I felt like there was something off, but I didn't consider that it might be me."

"Yeah. Same. I didn't think about it until we're sitting here and trying to figure out what it was. Obviously I'm not used to my son and your daughter talking to each other. I never thought they would get back together."

"Me either. So I guess it's kind of shocking that they are, and it's only natural that I would think that there's something weird about that."

"Exactly. That's what I was thinking too."

They were quiet for a moment, and then Gita said, "You really think that's it?"

"I'm not sure. It felt…a little contrived, but maybe it's because I was feeling guilty too. I do feel somewhat guilty."

"Because we're not being honest?"

"Yeah. We're deceiving people, and it doesn't feel right."

"I've been shoving that thought aside, because we're helping people, Grace and Trevor, and they deserve it. But… You're right. It doesn't feel good to know I'm not being honest."

"Maybe we should confess exactly what's going on when we're on the kayak trip. We'll have lots of time together to talk about it, and we can get far enough away from them that they won't be able to hear us."

"Just be careful, because you remember how well sound travels over the water, and no matter how far we are, if the atmosphere is right, they're going to be able to hear us plain as day."

"I'll keep that in mind. Maybe between now and then, we can suggest taking a picnic along, so we'll be sure to have time alone. Plenty of it where we can compare notes and come clean."

"Is it terrible that I don't really want to?" Gita asked softly. She didn't really want to examine that at all, and she held her breath before Don began to speak.

"I don't want to either. Mostly because…I want for you and I to have a real relationship."

"Really?" Gita said, even softer. Her heart skipped a beat and then started to beat happily in her chest.

"Yeah. Really." There was silence on the line as Gita tried to figure out what to say, but Don spoke first. "Gita Baby?"

Her heart thrilled as he said the nickname that only he called her. "Yes?"

"I think I'm too old to know all the right words. I don't know how the kids say this anymore, but back when we were in high school, I would be asking you to go with me right now. But that's not all I want. I… I feel like I don't know how long either one of us have left, but I'd like to spend all my time with you."

Was he asking her to marry him? She wasn't quite sure about that.

But she understood the idea of going with someone. That's what they did in high school. That was so long ago, and surely the kids didn't call it that anymore.

"So you're asking me to go with you?"

"I am, but I'm not playing. I... I'm going to want to marry you if you say yes to this, I'm just not sure that we ought not to wait a little bit longer. So we don't shock the entire town and overwhelm the Blueberry Beach hospital with heart attacks."

She laughed a little, even though heart attacks were not funny. It was the idea that two old geezers like Don and she could shock an entire town. But he was right, they would if they got married that suddenly. They were both known as reasonable, rational adults.

"Then my answer is yes. Yes, I'll go with you. Let's be official."

"All right. That sounds good, Gita Baby."

"And we can still go on the kayaking trip, and we can admit to what we've done, but then we can tell them that we decided that instead of having a fake relationship, we want a real one."

"Perfect."

Seventeen

L ater that week, Grace slipped out of the house to go for a walk along the beach as her mom lay down for a nap.

Her mom was getting better and better every single day, but she still took an hour or two nap in the afternoon. She said it was the effects of the anesthesia from the surgery. That her doctor had told her it could take weeks for the effects to wear off completely.

Grace wasn't sure exactly what it was. There was a part of her that was afraid that it was just her mom growing older. Slowing down. Tiring out easier.

But she wanted to believe what her mom said about the anesthesia and the effects, so she smiled and nodded and let her mom know that she would be taking a walk, and as always, her mom promised that she wouldn't get up while she was gone.

Her sisters had checked in periodically and were satisfied that Grace was taking good care of their mom and that their mom was getting better.

They hadn't stopped in over the weekend, but they had promised, both of them, to come the next weekend.

As far as Grace knew, they didn't know about their mom and Don, and they definitely didn't know about Grace and Trevor.

Grace wasn't looking forward to that reunion with her sisters. She would have to come clean about pretending that she and Trevor were a couple. It had morphed into that without her really expecting it to.

He had gone along with it, which she appreciated but then felt guilty for, because she was pretty sure that he didn't really want to. But it felt like he had to in order to back up what she had said.

She had all of that going through her mind as she walked down the street, past the healing garden. She was tempted to turn in and sit down there. She didn't want to though, because she wanted to get some exercise. Not only was it important for her mom to exercise, but it was important for her to as well. It was too easy to just sit at home and take care of her mom, and neglect her own health.

She'd never been very big on exercising, but the older she got, the more she knew if she wanted to stay active and healthy, she needed to take care of herself, and exercising was a part of that.

Regardless, there were about sixty different things jumbled up in her head that she was trying to figure out and think about, but she couldn't make heads or tails of them, and so she finally gave up altogether and lifted her face to the lake breeze. It was a beautiful spring day, and the waves were coming in with regularity. She loved the sound, soothing and eternal, and the sparkling blue under the warming sun reminded her of every single spring of her youth.

She hadn't walked far when she saw two horses being ridden her way.

They were beautiful, large Clydesdales, the kind that a person typically saw hooked to a cart or wagon, but these were being ridden.

She knew immediately that it was Becky and Rodney exercising their horses. Her mama talked a good bit about what Rodney and Becky were doing in Raspberry Ridge and about what a beautiful love story they had.

The thought of their sweet, second chance romance warmed Grace, but it also made her slightly bittersweet. Her own love story, which had begun in high school, had taken a turn for the worse, when she had left the one she should have stayed with and married the wrong man for all the wrong reasons. Her ex was the kind of man who was charismatic and successful and attractive, and she got sucked into believing his lies.

Some he outright told, but more that he insinuated. That he was rich and successful and that she would be rich and successful by going along with him.

For some reason, that had been so important to her ten years ago. Why? Why did that matter so much?

She couldn't figure her younger self out. Hadn't she realized how important it was to find people who had integrity and character and to develop relationships with them? How could she have thought that things like that were so unimportant, when they were the most important things of all?

"Beautiful day," Becky said as she reined her horse in. It stomped on the ground and tossed its head and was so huge that if Becky hadn't controlled it so expertly, Grace would have been scared.

Rodney stopped beside her, and his horse was slightly bigger, although equally as regal and beautiful.

"It sure is. And seeing your horses makes it even better," Grace said.

"Come over sometime, and we'll take a ride together," Becky offered.

"I'd love to, but you have to start out with lessons, because as much as I've always admired horses, I've never gotten to ride."

A love for horses was something that was very common for girls as she was growing up. But living by the lake as they did, there wasn't much opportunity to ride and even less to own one. Although she knew there were several stables down the beach now. If there were horses there when she was growing up, she hadn't known about them. And considering that her dad had been a hand on a fishing boat, and her mom had been a stay-at-home mom other than her crafts which she sold in magazines and newspapers and in festivals during the summer, they hadn't had much money.

"I'm more than happy to give you lessons anytime. Just stop in. You can call first if you want to, but we're not doing anything so pressing that I wouldn't have ten or fifteen minutes to do a lesson as long as we can find someone to watch the twins for us."

"I appreciate it. I'd really love to ride. Could I bring someone with me so I'm not alone?" She knew that sounded kind of cowardly, and Becky was a sweetheart. It wasn't like she was scary to be around, but

Grace didn't want to be the only incompetent person. And Becky seemed to understand. She smiled anyway and nodded her head.

"Of course. Bring a friend. We've got multiple horses, and you're welcome to use any that you'd like."

"Thank you so much. I'll keep that in mind."

She wondered if all four of them could go, her mom and Don and Trevor. That would be another thing they could do as a date.

She thought about asking but just lifted her hand in a wave and smiled instead as Becky and Rodney looked at each other, a look of love and understanding and of total oneness passing between them.

It was the kind of look that made her a little jealous. After all, she could have had that with Trevor, she was sure of it. But she'd been dumb and childish and immature in her youth.

They rode off, and Grace continued down the beach. As she thought about Becky and Rodney and mistakes she made in her past, she realized that she was spending an inordinate amount of time regretting her mistakes rather than learning from them. At that point, she decided that instead of just thinking about calling her friends, when she got home, she was going to look up their numbers and actually do it. She might not have made the best decisions when she was younger, but she could correct that now by trying to place the importance on other people that they deserved in her life.

That included Trevor, too, although she wasn't exactly sure what that looked like, since she didn't have to call him. She'd already spoken with him. But... Did that mean developing a relationship with him? Or keeping the relationship that they had platonic, so she didn't make any major mistakes?

She wasn't exactly sure, but one thing she was absolutely certain about, it was long past time for her to get over the past and to reach out to the people that she'd been avoiding.

Eighteen

"Did you talk to Gita since she had her physical therapy?" Trevor asked as he carefully glued another piece of wood onto the music box he was making.

"I did. She's been cleared to go to kayaking. They still want her to take it easy, but they said the more she exercises, the better. They want her to stay active, and she told me that she thought that they were pretty excited that she was planning something as adventurous as a kayak trip."

"Good. So we're on for Friday then?"

"Sure."

It was only two days away but felt like forever. It had been last Wednesday when they had last eaten at Gita and Grace's house. He knew that it was going to be this week until he saw Grace again, unless he specifically asked her to do something else, but that seemed to go against what they had agreed on, which was to do the kayak trip next.

He wasn't sure their relationship was at the point where he could tell her that he wanted to do more. That he longed to see her when she wasn't around and thought about her almost constantly.

"Are you good to finish up in here? I'll go on up to the house and finish getting supper ready."

"Sure. I'll be up in about fifteen minutes and will give you a hand."

He looked around the workbench. He didn't like to leave it when it wasn't cleaned up. "As soon as I finish putting everything away."

"No rush. You can finish what you're working on."

"Almost done. I'm at a good stopping point and will pick it up tomorrow."

Part of the reason he moved back was so that he could spend time with his dad. He didn't want his dad to have to make supper by himself all the time. Once in a while was fine, but he'd done it by himself the day before and also brought lunch out to the workshop.

Trevor had a tendency to get lost in his work, especially when he was doing his best to try not to think about Grace. Of course, maybe that was just an excuse. But he didn't think so. He really was trying to distract himself with work. If Grace were at the house, he would be hard-pressed to keep himself out of it.

He felt like a teenager. Surely that type of thing would wear off.

The door closed behind his dad, and he tried to clear his mind of thoughts of Grace, and how he could spend more time with her, and what he could do to impress her.

Was that what he wanted to do? Impress her? Because it seemed like in high school, she had been so underwhelmed by him that she had been able to run off without any trouble at all. Leaving him behind like the rest of her hometown.

Maybe that wasn't quite fair, but that's what it felt like.

He still hadn't figured out a way to capture her attention and make her see him for more than the hometown boy she left behind some years ago, when something white and slightly faded, something that looked like writing paper, caught his eye from between the workbench and the wall.

That was odd. His dad and he were the only people who came in here, and he'd never seen his dad writing anything down on a piece of paper. He might write something on his hand or on the edge of the newspaper, back when they still got one, but if his dad owned a notebook, Trevor didn't know anything about it.

Maybe it was from the person who used to own the house before them. But his dad had owned it all of his life. More than three decades of homeownership.

It might be something from his mom.

And with that, he looked around until he found a pair of tweezers and was able to grab a hold of whatever it was and slide it out from between the wall and the workbench.

It turned out to be two pieces of paper.

He opened both. One was dated for just after his mother had left his dad. The other was dated about six months prior.

He read the one that was almost five years old first.

It was his dad, writing to his mom and begging her to come back. It was hard to read, and Trevor almost folded it and put it away, because he knew that the words were not for his eyes.

He hadn't realized how broken up his dad was. He'd come and visited him, sure. He'd invited him to Chicago, and his dad had gone, taking off from work and hanging out at Trevor's rented apartment. Still, the grief that just poured off the page, the absolute desire to have his wife back, the pain, the baffled confusion where his dad didn't understand what he had done wrong that would cause his wife to take off and leave him. It was all there, evident, and almost eloquently said. He hadn't known Dad was such a great writer. But at the bottom of the letter, it was signed, "your devoted husband, Don."

Trevor swallowed, not realizing tears had come to his eyes, and his throat tightened until the paper in his hand lowered and rested on the workbench, crinkling slightly.

He almost folded it up and walked away without reading the other one. He really didn't want to know. But he found himself curious. Had his dad healed at all in the last five years? Was the second letter a letter of acceptance?

He wasn't sure and found himself more curious than ashamed that he had pried into his dad's private affairs.

He took the other letter, flattened it with his hand, and then started to read.

His heart untwisted and loosened along with his stomach as he made his way down through the letter. This one was shorter but no less filled with the raw feelings of his father.

This one was thanking his wife for the lessons she had taught him. For the hard thing that she had placed in his life. For not coming back, for showing him that he didn't need her like he thought, because he'd found out that God was enough, more than what he needed.

It was a letter almost of praise, coming from the heart of a man who had grown and become better because of the trial that he'd been through.

Was his dad really thankful that his mother had left?

Toward the end, his dad wondered, almost as though he wasn't talking to his wife anymore, as to whether he would ever love again. The idea that he would give so much of himself to another human scared him, and Trevor understood the feeling. The idea of making oneself vulnerable to someone else, knowing that all they had to do was go back on their word, and they could inflict pain upon him the likes of which he hadn't felt before.

But Don ended the letter by saying that yes, yes, he thought he could. Because he learned from the first time that God was in control. Even when it didn't feel like it. And that doing the right thing always made a person feel better in the end. He didn't exactly castigate his wife for leaving, but he mentioned that he had never regretted keeping his vows. And he wouldn't regret finding someone else. Someone to share his life with, someone to make their lives better.

He also thanked her for showing him areas where he could become better. Not that he was taking the blame for the fact that his wife had left him, but he realized that he could have been a better husband. He could have been more responsive and attentive. He could have spent less time in front of the television and more time doing something with his wife.

He thanked her for those lessons. Thanked her for making him realize that while it wasn't up to him to make anyone stay with him, it was up to him to be the kind of human being that a woman wanted to be with. Who she was happy to be with, and if there was something that he could do to make his marriage better, then by all means, he would do it. Whereas before, he had not thought like that at all.

Trevor ran his hand down over the letter. This one was signed, "Love, Don."

They had been divorced for a while by that point in time, and there was no hope of getting her back. He didn't even suggest it.

The five years had made a big difference in his dad's life. But only because his dad had chosen to see the trial that he'd gone through as something he could learn from and become better through.

He supposed he could have seen it as ruining his life, as tearing his life apart at the seams, and seeing that he would never have everything he wanted.

Instead, he'd made the decisions to learn the lessons that God had for him to learn, then to put them in practice.

There had been a definite change in his dad over the last five years, but Trevor had spent so much time with him, it wasn't obvious until now. He was no longer bitter and angry and sad, but instead he was happy and grateful. Funny and eager to live life.

Maybe that was why he and Gita were getting along so well.

He supposed there were lessons in there for him, but he wasn't sure exactly what they were, since he'd never had a wife divorce him or leave him for another man.

Except, Grace kind of had. She didn't cheat on him. She'd left and wasn't in a relationship with anyone. Still, she'd made him feel like he wasn't enough, like he needed to figure out what he could do to impress her, instead of only thinking that whatever character and integrity he had should be enough. And if she wasn't impressed by that, then he didn't need to worry about it. Was that right? He felt like it was.

Carefully putting the letters back where he found them, he wondered if he should tell his dad that he had discovered them and gotten them out. But then he'd have to admit that he had read them and pried into something that maybe he shouldn't have. Except, the lessons contained in those letters were valuable and helpful.

He decided if the opportunity ever came up, he'd tell his dad what he found and thank him for writing them since it had been a blessing. But he wasn't going to bring the subject up himself.

His dad had gone through something hard, difficult, something that most people never had to go through, and he'd come out better.

Trevor had gone through something similar, when Grace had left, and now she was back. Had he handled it as well as he could? Were there still lessons he needed to learn? He'd have to think about that.

Nineteen

"It's such a beautiful day," Grace said as they lifted one of the two rented double kayaks from the back of Trevor's truck.

There was no way to drive to the beach at Raspberry Ridge, but on up the road a short distance at Blackberry Bay, there was not just a way to get kayaks in the water but also a nice peaceful cove which was perfect for kayaking. Even if a sudden spring storm came up, which they checked the weather and there wasn't supposed to be, there were plenty of places where they could get out of the water. Plus, the water would not be nearly as rough as the regular lake water.

Blackberry Bay was perfect for kayaking.

She needed to do this more often. It was only a few minutes away from her house.

"It's a gorgeous day. It makes me wonder why you haven't bought a kayak up until this point."

She laughed. "I was wondering the same thing. They're expensive, but as many times as I've rented them, I could have bought one long ago."

"Then you have to find a place to store it and make sure you don't lose the paddles and everything. If you rent it, all responsibility is on someone else. Sometimes that's nice."

She nodded, looking at him thoughtfully. There seemed to be something that had shifted in his personality since she had seen him last. "Yes. All the responsibility is on someone else. Isn't it nice when that happens?"

She smiled at him as he looked at her. They had talked a couple of times on the phone, but not for long, and they hadn't made any more plans. She realized now that maybe they should have. At least figured out what they could suggest for their parents to do next to keep them together.

"My goodness. I remember doing this with you girls when you were little, but I don't think I've done it in twenty years."

Gita looked like she was having the time of her life. Her yoga pants emphasized her slender legs, and she wasn't moving like someone who had just had hip replacement less than four weeks ago.

"Trevor and I go a good bit. Although this is the first time this spring we've been out. This time of year, you have to watch for those sudden spring storms popping up."

"I know. I kept checking the weather, and everything is clear, but you just never know."

"I don't think we need to worry about that too much. As long as we stay in Blackberry Bay, we'll be able to get out of the water easily. Even if something comes up suddenly, the water here doesn't get nearly as choppy as it does out on the lake." Trevor sounded confident, as well he should, if he was out kayaking as much as Don said they were.

"If you want to get in, you can, and I'll push the kayak out in the water so you don't have to get wet," Trevor offered as he set their kayak down in the water.

Don was doing the same for Gita, and Grace said, "Can you hold on one second. Please?"

He nodded, and she hurried over to offer a hand to her mother to help steady her.

"I know you're almost as good as new, but it'll make me feel a little better if I give you a hand till you get in the boat."

"I'm glad you did. I've been doing my exercises religiously, way more than what they asked me to, but I still don't feel like I have my balance completely back."

"That's what your therapist said was important," Grace said, and Gita nodded, like that's exactly what she had been thinking about.

Grace held a hand out, and her mom placed hers in it. She put first one foot and then the other into the boat.

"I'm holding it as steady as I can," Don said as the boat rocked just a little, and Grace moved another hand to help her mom steady herself.

Finally, her mom was settled in the boat. Grace thought about offering to help Don but figured he would be insulted.

Instead, she went back to her own boat.

"Thanks. I know she probably would have been fine, but..." She shrugged a little.

"I like seeing you take care of your mom. It makes me happy in some elemental way. I know that's weird."

"I don't think that's weird. It makes me happy to see you taking care of your dad. It's what kids are supposed to do."

"It's weird when that kind of flip-flops, you know? Where you realize that your parents need you, and it's not just you doing something good, it's you doing something necessary."

"Yeah. I've been seeing that more and more. It's hard for me to imagine my mom not being the strong, capable woman that she's always been, but you're right. There comes a time when that shift happens, and that's what we get."

"I don't necessarily think that's a bad thing. It teaches kids to think about what their parents did for them and to be grateful. It also teaches you to think beyond yourself. A lot of times with our parents, we're always thinking about what they can do for us, and it's good for us to start thinking about what we can do for them."

"Yeah. I suppose that does grow you, along with a lot of other things," she said, thinking about the discussion that they'd had before where they talked about trials making them better people.

"I'm really looking forward to this today," he said as he held out a hand to help her into the kayak.

She glanced at it, trying not to take too long but remembering when it used to be her right to hold that hand. When that hand had comforted her and sat gently on her back or on her thigh. When they walked down the street casually clasping hands and laughing together.

There were so many memories bound up in that hand.

She knew she hesitated a second or two too long, but she put her hand in his without further comment.

He helped her in the boat, and he didn't say anything either.

Kayaking was something they hadn't done when they were together, although she wasn't sure why. It was a fun activity that they both enjoyed.

"I'm in," she said as she settled down on her seat. She wished there was something she could do to help him and put her oar in the water, figuring that she could at least try to ballast the boat as he moved it into the deeper water, so when he set it down, the underside didn't scrape on the bottom.

"I'm fine. Brace yourself, because it might wobble a bit when I get in."

She noted that Don had gotten in without any major issues, meaning that her mother was still dry, as was he.

The physical therapist had told them that swimming would not hurt her, but she should continue to make a concerted effort to not fall down.

The kayak shook as Trevor got in behind her, and she did what she could to keep it steady, although she wasn't sure whether she was actually helping anything or not. Despite growing up by the lake, she wasn't that great at being on the water.

A tendril of nervousness, coupled with fear, tightened in the pit of her stomach, and she remembered why she didn't kayak despite being so close to the lake.

She wasn't going to think about that today. She hadn't thought about it when they suggested the outing; it had been nothing but a fun trip. And that's the way she wanted to keep it. She wasn't going to keep living her life constantly thinking about the past and allowing it and the fear it brought to control her.

"I'm in. That wasn't as bad as it could have been. I don't know how many times I've capsized my kayak getting in and out. Of course, that was back when I was just learning."

"I've capsized mine multiple times too. It's not bad in the summer when it's warm out. It's nice today, but I don't think I want to go for a swim if I can keep from it."

"I'm in agreement with that. When I was younger, I might have disagreed with you, but at this point in my life, I know I would be cold and miserable for the rest of the day. Or at least until my clothes dried out enough that I could feel like I was warm."

"Sometimes I would get wet and wouldn't be warm the rest of the day. So, especially if clouds come up and it starts to get windy."

"True. And I don't expect that to happen today, but that would generally keep me from getting warm again."

"Of course, nothing makes a hot shower feel better than to be freezing for the six hours prior to it."

"Good point," he said good-naturedly.

She didn't like sitting in front of him where they couldn't see each other. She'd rather turn around so they could face each other, but that wasn't the way the kayaks were made.

Gita and Don were out ahead of them about fifty yards and seemed to be chatting and enjoying themselves.

They were quiet for a bit with just the dipping of the oars, and while they could hear their parents talking, they couldn't hear what they were saying.

"What you said about voices carrying, I can hear them but can't make them out. I think we're safe to talk if you need to." Trevor's voice came low and soft behind her.

"I was thinking the same thing," she said, smiling, although he couldn't see her.

"Good. I feel like our parents are moving closer without us even doing anything," he said. "I know they talk on the phone every night, and a lot of times, he'll mention that he's talked with her in the morning before I get back from my jog."

She hadn't realized that he ran in the morning. And she found that almost as interesting, maybe more so, than knowing that their parents talked so much.

"I guess I knew that. I wonder what in the world they could have to talk about. But they seem to discuss pretty much anything and everything."

"I think that's what the best relationships do. They are interested in each other's opinions and listen. Conversation really does seem to bring people closer together." She could hear him sigh. Even though the strokes were slow, the rhythmic splashes of his paddle never wavered. They fell into a rhythm that worked for both of them, and she wasn't sure she'd ever kayaked with someone who got her so quickly and easily.

"I might not have admitted that when I was younger. I thought... other things...were more important in a relationship. A romantic one anyway."

She grinned a little and then was kind of glad that her back was to him, because she didn't think before she asked the next question. "What were other things?" Even though she thought she knew the answer.

He huffed a little. "A teenage boy, hormones, need I say any more?"

She laughed. "I guess I would say that's important too. But I definitely think that the talking probably gets left by the wayside more than that."

"I think that's spoken like a woman. Because, from my perspective, *that*," he said, emphasizing the word with a humor that made her smile, "is probably more important to a man than talking."

"Really?" She wasn't sure she agreed with that, but she wasn't a man, so her opinion was hardly expert or even semi-knowledgeable.

"Yeah. Really. I agree about talking. Although so many times we hear about communication, and I don't really see that as a necessity. I see it as important, but not more important than kindness, consideration, and even sacrifice. A lack of pride, a desire to put the other first. Those are all things we read about in the Bible. Communication isn't really in there."

"Good point. But *that*," she emphasized "that" the way he had, and she could practically feel him smiling, "is."

"It sure is," he agreed and didn't say anything more.

"I'm not sure how we got on that subject, though, because we were talking about our parents."

"Yeah. And saying how they had the communication thing down, but I'm not sure about *that*."

"Oh. No. Don't. Please. We are not going to discuss our parents and *that* in the same sentence." She gave an exaggerated shiver, which she really didn't have to fake.

"That is something we agree on," he said. And was quiet for a bit.

"I feel a little bit guilty," she said.

"Why?" he asked right away.

"Because my mom has asked me multiple times how our relationship is going, and... I've been on the verge of admitting that we don't really have one."

"It's made me feel uncomfortable as well, although my dad hasn't asked. I guess that's the difference between men and women."

"Possibly. But yeah, I've been on the hot seat a couple of times, and... I don't like lying. Or deceiving. And I feel like I've been on the verge of having to do both multiple times."

"I guess the remedy for that is to come clean." The oars dipped in and pushed twice more before he spoke again. "I don't like the idea of the guilt, although I love the idea of the fact that our parents are closer now than they were."

"Same. But I honestly think that we could probably lay off and they'll be fine. I think they like each other well enough that they don't need us anymore."

"If they even did to begin with."

"Good point. I've spent a little bit of time wondering if they were together because of us, or if I was just giving myself more credit than I deserve."

"That is a legitimate question."

They were quiet again with just the dip of the paddle and the occasional sound of their parents' laughter carrying across the water. They didn't stay right with them but gave them privacy and space.

"Can I ask you a question?"

"You just did," she said easily, smiling, because she always thought it was funny when someone asked if they could ask a question.

"Sorry. I'll take that as a yes. Although, you might not appreciate me prying. Maybe I should have specified it's a personal question."

"Go right ahead." She didn't know that everything in her life was an open book, but she couldn't think of anything off the top of her head that she wouldn't be willing to discuss with Trevor.

"How long did it take you to get back on the water?"

She knew exactly what he was referring to. "It was the year after. I didn't go back in the rest of that summer. And I didn't want to go in the summer after, but... My mom really thought it was important that I did. I'm glad she made me, because growing up beside the lake, there's so much enjoyment there. But... I would never do it without a life vest."

"We shouldn't have to begin with."

"Standards were different back then. We weren't doing anything everybody else didn't do. Not that I'm defending it, because I agree, it's just...it wasn't like we were being rebellious."

"Yeah. That was the incident that made me determined that I would never go on the lake without one."

"I never figured out what happened," she said.

He didn't pry, and she appreciated that. She didn't want to rehash everything while they were in kayaks on the water. The water underneath them wasn't deep, but it was well over their heads and measured in dozens of feet rather than single digits.

"I guess I have another question similar to that one."

Similar to how did she ever get back in the water again? Or how long did it take her to get back in the water?

"Okay," she said, leaving it open-ended so that he could ask whatever he wanted.

"How long do you think it'll take you before you're ready to date again?"

Whoa. That was unexpected. It took a minute for her to shift gears in her head.

It wasn't that she hadn't thought of dating again. She just...hadn't thought about it lately.

"When it first happened, I didn't think I would ever date again. I... don't think I ever wanted to beg my husband to take me back. After all, he cheated on me, and I really didn't want to go back. But I wanted him to not cheat, you know? To take it all back. I wanted to find out that it was wrong, not true. I wanted to die at times too." She said the last bit very softly, because it wasn't something she discussed with just anyone. In fact, Trevor was the first person she had mentioned it to outside of the counselor that she'd gone to for five sessions before she quit.

"I think I can understand. I can't even imagine how terrible it must have been."

"You know a little bit, because I did it to you. Sometimes I wondered if I was reaping what I sowed. I never cheated on you. I promise you that. But I did leave, and my focus was on me, and I didn't think a whole lot about how I was hurting you."

"It did hurt. I felt like...I wasn't worth anything. I wondered what was wrong with me that you wouldn't love me. That I was such an easy thing to toss aside."

"You weren't. I thought of you for a long time after I left. Even when I started dating the man I eventually married, he never measured up to you. But I was determined in my heart that I would never go back. It...took a lot to bring me back to Raspberry Ridge. God really had to pile it on me before I saw the light."

"I guess you're stubborn."

"That's one way of looking at it." She laughed a little, even though she wondered if she had gone back to Raspberry Ridge immediately, if she would have been able to avoid all the pain. But then she would have avoided the lessons too, and they'd already had that discussion.

"You didn't really answer my question." He spoke after they'd been quiet for a bit.

"I guess I don't know how to answer. I told you, at first I was determined that I would never..." She let her words trail off. How was she going to tell him that he was the first, and most likely only, person she would even consider dating after what happened?

That after being married to the man she had been married to, he looked so much better than anyone she even knew. To have a man of character and convictions, who was also considerate and kind, who took care of his dad, and who made sure that he took care of her as well. Who cared about honesty and integrity and didn't care what other people thought of him. Except for her, apparently.

"Now?" He prompted after her voice trailed off and she didn't start speaking again.

"And now, I guess for the right person, I'm ready." She took a deep breath, continuing to paddle, thinking, and choosing her words carefully. "I thought about this a lot. I know people whose spouse has cheated on them, and they would never have guessed it. With mine, I think I should have seen the handwriting on the wall. I should have known before I even married him that he wasn't a good person. But I know preachers who have cheated on their wives. Pastor's wives who cheated on their husbands. Good people, people that no one thinks would ever do anything wrong, who abandoned their spouse and family, either with someone else or just because they couldn't take it anymore, I guess. I don't think there's any way to know. In life, we just don't get a guarantee."

"That's it. The truth. We don't get a guarantee."

"No. We don't get a guarantee that we are going to be happy, that life is going to be easy, that people are going to do what we want them to do, that they're not going to hurt us, that we're not going to get sick, that our family isn't going to suffer, that we won't have friends who are going to die, or that we're not going to go through tragedy. There is no guarantee. The only guarantee we have is that God is with us. And that He's going to work everything out for our good and His glory."

"Yeah. You're right." He swallowed and then said, "That, and if we're faithful, our reward is in heaven. That's a guarantee too."

"Right. We don't have a promise of earthly riches. While we do have the promise of a heavenly reward."

"Exactly. You're right. I think we go through life thinking that we should have a guarantee. That somehow God owes us peace and tranquility and blessing and ease and all those other things, but He doesn't. He just doesn't."

"No. And I suppose that's a roundabout way of saying that at first I decided I was never going to date again because how can I trust someone?" She let out a breath. "And then I realized that I can trust someone just as easily as I did before, because I have just as much guarantee—none—about the person being faithful as I did before. It's just a matter of making sure that I'm with the person God wants me to be with. But even then, that person might do things that they shouldn't, even though I'm completely in God's will. Does that make sense?"

"Yeah. It does, although I've never seen it like that before."

They were quiet for a bit. They'd gotten to the edge of Blackberry Bay, where the sheltered area met the wider expanse of the lake. They needed to turn around. The way they were facing, Grace had to turn her head and look past Trevor sitting behind her in order to see her mom and his dad. She didn't do that. She looked out on the lake, thinking about all the tragedy that it had seen but how that was tempered by all the beautiful things it had been witness to as well. People getting married on the shores, families vacationing and enjoying the water and waves and the sun and the fun.

Sure, there had been shipwrecks and tragedies like she'd endured, but the good always outweighed the bad. Always. It was just a matter of perspective.

"I think it's time to turn around. My stomach is growling and feels like it's time to eat," he said after they slowly drifted forward for a while, without saying anything. It seemed both of them were enjoying the warm sun on their faces and the cool breeze, as well as the peacefulness of the water. There was just something about being on the water that was soothing and grounding.

"I think you're right. I'm thirsty anyway."

"I have water back in the cooler, or I have a warm one here."

"I can wait," she said as they started to turn their kayak.

As they turned, she saw that their parents had already made it to shore and had found a nice site for them to eat their picnic lunch. The cooler was in their kayak, but the basket with the blanket and some nonperishables were with them.

"They're so cute together," Grace said as Don held his arm out for Gita, and she took it. He steadied her and helped her climb up the bank. It wasn't super steep, but to see them taking care of each other like that just made her heart happy.

"My dad really is infatuated, I think. I feel like their relationship might be moving pretty quickly. We could hear wedding bells by the end of this year, maybe even sooner."

"Do you really think so?" Grace asked, shocked. Of course, she realized that they were truly serious about each other, but as far as she knew, her mom hadn't even told her sisters yet.

"Sure. Don't you think?"

"I don't know. I mean, my sisters are coming on Saturday, and I think that's when Mom is going to tell them. It's a little crazy to think that they could be married...married."

"I didn't mean to shock you like that. But look at them. They're...so in love."

"No question. And I don't think Mom could have found a better person. Your dad's pretty awesome, even if he does call her Gita Baby."

"Doesn't she like it?"

"I think she loves it. To be honest, it makes me cringe every time I hear it, but then to see my mom's face, and the love on it, and the adoration... He knows exactly what she wants, and he's given it to her."

"I think my dad learned a lot from my mom leaving." It seemed like he had more to say, but he closed his mouth, and they didn't talk about it anymore, rowing toward their parents, the kayak hitting the edge of the bank. Grace was able to jump up and get out without getting wet.

She turned around and grabbed a hold of the rope, keeping the kayak on the bank as Trevor got off.

"Thanks. I can pull it out of the water," he said.

"I'll give you a hand. Because there is enough stuff in the back for both of us to carry up. Maybe we'll only have to make one trip if we both do it."

"All right. Thanks," he said.

They pulled the kayak out of the water and got the cooler which contained their drinks and the meat to make sandwiches, along with some vegetables Grace and her mom had cut up earlier that morning.

It was such a happy, fun time as they laughed and carried things up. Trevor said something about working up an appetite and how Grace's muscles were going to look like a bodybuilder's, since he made her do most of the work, and Gita had laughed and made a muscle and said that she was going to look like a bodybuilder too.

They spread the food out on the blanket, settling down on the ground, with Trevor saying grace before they ate.

Grace didn't think a day could get any more perfect.

Twenty

Gita bit her lip. She and Don had put off telling Grace and Trevor long enough. The food was long since eaten, and they'd gathered up their garbage but had lingered at the blanket, waiting for an opening.

Grace and Trevor seemed to be sharing secret smiles and looks that encouraged Gita, although she felt like if they just kept things going a little bit longer, they could know without a doubt that Grace and Trevor were well on their way to the relationship that they'd lost back when they were younger.

But she agreed with Don—she didn't want to keep deceiving them. She had just decided that she was going to open her mouth and just spit it out, when Grace smiled at Trevor, and he nodded his head. And then she said, "I have something to confess."

"We have something to confess," Trevor corrected her, emphasizing the "we."

"That sounds serious," Don said, not looking like he thought it was serious at all. He leaned on one elbow, lying on his side. Gita had a little chair, and she sat on the blanket. He had his hand over top of hers on the arm of her chair.

When he spoke, he squeezed her hand.

"It's funny you should mention it, because Don and I have

something we'd like to confess as well," she said, watching her daughter carefully. Grace's eyes opened wide, as though she were surprised, while Trevor's eyes narrowed, as though he was speculating on what it could be.

"All right. You go first," Grace said.

"No. I just wanted to let you know that we had something that we need to confess, so don't go running off. But you said it first, so you can go ahead and say whatever it is that you need to say."

"All right." Grace took a breath, looked at Trevor, as though she were needing a little bit of extra courage, and then she seemed to decide that she just needed to say it. "Trevor and I were pretending to be a couple because we wanted to give you guys an opportunity to be together, because we thought that if you guys were together enough, you would fall in love."

She looked at Trevor, who nodded and then said, "It's like she said. We...deceived you. Basically, lied." He took a breath, and then he said, "I'm sorry. I think it was mostly my idea, and it wasn't a good one. I'm ashamed, in any event."

"Me too. I'm sorry, and it wasn't Trevor's idea. It was mine. I wanted to play matchmaker, because I wanted you guys to get together and be happy, and that seemed like a good way." Grace shook her head and looked down at her hands in her lap.

Don cleared his throat. "Funny you should mention it."

He looked up at Gita, who didn't know what to say. She almost wanted to laugh. Maybe she would have, if it wasn't so serious, since they had been deceiving each other all this time. Except, she and Don were serious about their relationship, and they had that to say as well. But even though she waited a few moments, Grace and Trevor did not speak again.

"We forgive you. I can say that with confidence because we did the same thing." She started off, and then Don took over.

"The thing is, we thought that you guys had a solid relationship when you were younger, and thought maybe if you spent some time together, you would rekindle that. I saw Trevor looking happy when he was with Grace."

"And I thought Grace looked very happy when she was with Trevor. The two of you seem destined to be together."

"And we decided that we would pretend to have a relationship in order to get you to spend time together."

"Something didn't feel right about that," Grace said, and the look on her face said she felt validated for having the feeling. "I just thought it was because it was weird to see my mom with a man who wasn't my dad."

"But you two are together for real now," Trevor said slowly, looking at Don's hand sitting on top of Gita's on the arm of her chair.

She looked down, saw that his hand was there, and twisted hers until their palms met and their fingers twined together.

"You're right. We were the ones who were fooled. We thought we were going to get the two of you together, and we ended up falling in love with each other."

She smiled at Don. They'd talked about that in the kayak as they'd been paddling around the bay. They both admitted that they had fallen in love. They didn't know exactly what that meant at their age. It wasn't the giddy, completely oblivious love of their youth. It was a more mature feeling, more serious, but at the same time an almost desperate feeling, because life was short, and they knew it better now than they did back then.

"Wow. So... You two started out doing something that was a little deceitful, and then you ended up falling in love with each other?"

"That's right," Don said, looking at his son. "We started out wanting the best for you and being deceitful in order to get it. I'm sorry. I didn't mean to manipulate you, which, in hindsight, is what it was."

"I'm sorry too. I shouldn't have suggested it."

"I'm the one who suggested it," Don said, turning to her and arguing.

She smiled. "Is this something we're going to fight about?"

"We need to have our first fight at some point. This seems like as good a time as any."

"Should we do it in front of the children?"

"I resent being called a child," Trevor interrupted them.

"I guess that's a no. We'll need to take this to the kayak, Gita Baby,"

Don said, making her insides twirl as he used her nickname. She didn't think she would ever get tired of hearing it.

"All right. A truce for now; we'll fight later," Gita said. Wanting to agree with whatever he said. There was nothing that was so important that she would fight over it. They agreed about the important things, God and character, and everything else could be a compromise at some point.

"So, what are you two?"

"Us?" Grace asked, looking like a deer caught in headlights.

"Yeah," Don said. "We've admitted that we were deceitful, but it bit us, and something happened that we weren't expecting. We fell in love," he said, looking at Gita with a look of admiration that made her insides twirl.

"That's right. We did." She paused and then squeezed Don's hand as she looked back at Grace and Trevor. Grace looked scared, but Trevor looked thoughtful. "What about you?"

"No. That didn't happen at all," Grace said, and then she stood abruptly, making a show of brushing her lap off and looking around at the three who were still seated. "Are you guys ready to go?"

No one said anything for a moment, and then Gita took pity on her daughter. It was obvious she felt something but didn't want to admit it. Maybe she was scared, or maybe she was afraid that Trevor didn't feel the same.

Gita could disabuse her of that notion, but maybe that was something that she had to figure out on her own. That seemed to be the way love was. A person had to navigate the waters alone. Or at least navigate the waters with the Lord. She supposed it was more important to find someone who loved God and wanted to serve Him than it was to find someone a person was "in love" with. That was one of the things she had learned over her life.

"I'm ready," Gita said, sliding to the edge of her chair and standing up the way her therapist had taught her to.

Getting in and out of the kayak was a little bit of a stretch for her, but she didn't feel any pain at all, although she figured her muscles were probably going to be sore the next day and possibly for the next week.

"Same. I'm eager to get back on the water. I forgot how much I loved it," Don said as he pretended that there wasn't anything wrong and ignored the fact that Grace seemed to be paranoid that she might have to deal with her feelings. There wasn't anyone here who didn't understand or feel that at some point. When she was ready, she'd come around.

Trevor seemed disappointed, and Gita pitied him. He had been patient with Grace for years. Or maybe, he had been patient with Grace, waited on her for years, and now needed to be patient again.

She wanted to tell him to just keep waiting, that Grace would come around. That there never had been anyone Grace had looked at the way she looked at Trevor, but she knew as well as anyone that sometimes people didn't do what they should do, even when they knew it. Sometimes they chose the hard way, even when they knew it was going to be the hard way, or the less desirable way, or even the stupid way.

She didn't want to think Grace would do that yet again, but she knew from experience, from watching other people live their lives, that it was quite possible that Grace would do exactly that.

They folded everything up and went down to their kayaks, with Don being such a gentleman and holding her hand, helping her in, making sure she was comfortable.

He pushed the kayak out and got in beside her with Trevor pushing it the rest of the way out as they began to paddle.

"That was unexpected," Don said when they were far enough away from the shore that their voices wouldn't carry. They spoke low just in case.

"I feel so bad for Trevor."

"Grace was hurt really badly. I can understand that, and I see how it might be hard to trust again."

"You didn't have a problem."

"I have years on her. She just went through her divorce last year. I'm not sure I would have been ready to be with someone a year after my wife left."

"You were married a lot longer. You raised children together. There's a difference."

"Some people just love deep and hard and with their whole souls, and when it goes bad, it goes really bad, and it hurts clear down to their bones in a way that they just can't get away from."

"It sounds like you're speaking from experience." She wished to comfort him, help him through the pain. Feel it herself so he didn't have to.

"Yeah," he said quietly. "But once you get through the other side, you realize that it's probably the best thing that could happen to you."

"I hate to say that I'm glad it did, but you and I wouldn't be here together if it hadn't."

"That's true. And this has been one of the best days of my life. I hope I have a lot more days like this with you."

"I think we should plan on it."

He grunted in agreement, and they skimmed out over the water. Gita was thrilled to her soul with the way her own relationship was going, but her heart hurt for Grace, who obviously was having trouble seeing what was right in front of her.

Twenty-One

Trevor didn't say anything as they pushed the kayak back out into the water. What was there to say? Grace had said everything. The way she had completely denied that there might be anything between them had cut him to the quick. He had thought that they were developing something together, but obviously she didn't feel that way.

He'd been trying to dig beneath the surface a little bit and to figure out whether she might be ready today, but she'd answered that question loud and clear as well.

It seemed like with Grace, he was always too little, too late or something. Maybe he just wasn't the person for her. Maybe she could never love him the way he had loved her. He thought about her for years and hadn't spent much time interested in anyone else. Obviously he'd been wasting his time.

But what else was he to do? He just didn't find anyone else interesting. Didn't want to get to know them the way he wanted to know Grace. Didn't want to be with them the way he wanted to be with Grace.

It was hard when one loved someone who didn't love one back. When you wanted to be with someone who didn't want to be with you.

She is with you today.

He heard the voice in his head and realized it was right. Maybe he was sinking into the depths of despair for no reason. Maybe she had panicked and was afraid that she was going to have to declare something that she didn't want to.

He felt like he was grasping at straws.

"Sorry about back there," she finally said after they'd been in the kayak for at least ten minutes. The bay was wide, and they were only halfway across, out by themselves. He hadn't even tried to figure out where their parents were and keep up with them. He'd been too focused on the pain he felt.

"It's okay. You were just saying what you felt." The words came out, and they even sounded normal. But he didn't feel normal inside. He felt like he wanted to get away from her as fast as he could, but he had more kayaking to do. He could hardly tell his parents he wanted to cut out early. But maybe he could ask Grace if she wanted to.

"I panicked. I didn't want to say. I—"

"It's fine. You don't have to explain anything. You said what you did, and you have the right to say what you feel."

He didn't want to hear her flimsy explanations. And he definitely didn't want an apology. Another, *I'm sorry, Trevor, but you're just not the right man for me*, wasn't going to cut it right now. He wanted her to want him. As long as she didn't say she didn't, he didn't have to face the facts.

"Trevor—"

"Please just enjoy the quiet. It's a nice day out. We don't have to talk."

He knew he shouldn't do that. Communication is what kept relationships alive, right? He wasn't sure he bought into that, but this was something that they should hash out, if they were going to have a relationship. But what was he going to do? Be friends with the woman he was in love with from now until forever? He didn't want to talk just for that.

Thankfully, she didn't argue with him but stayed quiet. He sank into deep thoughts, thoughts of how much of his life he'd wasted mooning over someone who couldn't even admit that she had feelings for him in front of her mother and his dad. She'd been able to fake it, but when it came time to tell her real feelings, there wasn't anything there for him.

It wasn't until a particularly strong gust of wind hit the kayak and a wave almost flipped it over that he realized that the wind picked up and one of those quick summer storms was upon them.

"Head to the beach! Pull!" His words were clipped, his command immediate and without room for argument. It was because of the fear that rose up inside of him. She got caught on the water once back when he was younger, and he never wanted to have it happen again. His one thought was to get Grace to safety.

Of course, they both had a life vest on, but waves didn't necessarily care, and one couldn't float when a wave was descending on top of one's head.

He looked around and saw that his dad had already guided his boat to the beach and he and Gita were out and on the shore. They had a bit of a walk to get to the truck, and it wouldn't be easy to carry their kayak, but they were safe.

There was no time for Trevor and Grace to cut the whole way across the lake to where their vehicle was parked.

"We're going to get out right here," he said, indicating the nearest shore. She didn't turn around to look, just pulled with all her might. He guided the kayak so they hit the closest outcropping, which was close to two miles around the bay from the truck, just as the first big drops of rain started to fall.

"Perfect timing," she said.

He jumped up, hopped out of the kayak, and pulled it onto the beach a little more, so Grace could get off without getting her feet wet, although he didn't know why he bothered. They were going to get soaked.

"We can use the kayak as a bit of shelter from the rain, put it upside down over our heads," Grace said as she looked around. He had no idea of what she was looking for, but he had already figured they would use the kayak as shelter. Although, a strong gust of wind could take it off, and they'd be left to be lashed at by the wind and rain.

Big drops started to come down faster when Grace said, "There's two stumps about the right distance apart. We might be able to put it upside down over those."

He looked where she was pointing, and if he were picking out perfect stumps, those wouldn't be it. But they were better than anything else they had.

"All right." She helped him drag the kayak to the stumps, which wasn't far away, and indeed, they were almost the perfect distance apart. One end of the kayak stuck out about a foot over the side of one stump, but there was plenty of room for them to sit underneath. Their butts would get wet as the rain ran down over the ground, except Grace was pulling some kind of package out of a small kit that she had brought.

"This will keep the ground dry."

"Hurry up. It's not going to matter. We'll be soaked."

Indeed, the rain came down harder. He could hear it and see it on the lake, but the trees were sheltering them some right now.

She shook it out, and he managed to flip the kayak over. Then, she put the plastic sheet she got from her pack down, and they both ducked underneath the kayak, stepping on the plastic.

There was enough extra plastic left over that they could pick it up and hold it against the overturned side of the kayak, protecting them from the rain that came in on that side.

They were finally situated as the rain pounded around them, and he sat there for a moment before he looked at her. "That was a handy thing to bring."

"You know how it is, in school there's always these water safety courses, and for some reason when they mentioned this, it really wasn't for safety, it was more for convenience, but I ended up buying one at some point." She lifted a shoulder and smiled. "This is the first time I've ever used it. It probably won't go back into the pack nearly as nice as it came out."

He laughed. "They never do."

They were close, closer than he'd been to her in a long time. With her face just inches from his as they both sat hunched over underneath the kayak, the rain battering the plastic and making him feel like they were in a world of their own.

"About earlier," she started.

He shook his head and brought a finger up, putting it on her lips.

He shouldn't touch her. He wanted to keep it there.

Something flickered in her eyes, and he wondered if she was feeling something of the same, and then he knew she couldn't be. After all, she'd rejected him. Again. Rather brutally.

"Are you ever going to let me talk about it?" she asked, speaking around his finger.

Her hand came up, and she took his hand in hers, taking it away from her lips but holding it between them. Not letting go.

He had a good mind to pull his hand away. After all, he didn't want to get wrapped up in her charms and her spell any more than he already was. Not that she ever deliberately set about trapping him. He was the one who had allowed himself to be ensnared. He had enjoyed every moment that he spent with her and wanted more.

"I guess I don't see that there's anything to talk about," he said.

His words were soft, since he was speaking mere inches from her face. He could see the little puffs of air moving her bangs, the ones that were not plastered to her forehead.

"Then maybe we shouldn't talk," she said, and he wasn't sure exactly what she meant, until she started to lean forward, her free hand coming up and sliding around the nape of his neck, tugging gently.

He should resist her. Should rip away, but there really wasn't room, not to mention, he didn't want to. He wanted to just let her pull him forward, even though he knew this was going to make everything worse.

He'd kissed her plenty of times in high school back when they dated, but that had been more than a decade ago, and he wanted to kiss her now. To see if the memories he had were as good as the real thing.

Then, as her lips touched his, he stopped thinking about anything but kissing her, although he realized that his memories paled in comparison to the real thing.

It was a soft kiss, gentle, and full of more questions than answers, and that's how he felt when he lifted his head, searching her eyes, his hands coming up and touching her cheeks, rubbing against the soft skin there.

Why had she kissed him? Why had he allowed her to? That was an even better question. She'd already hurt him, quite badly. Devastatingly bad, really. That was years ago, of course, but now, just today, she hurt him again. How many rejections was he supposed to take? And yet, he allowed her to kiss him, knowing she didn't really want him.

Still, he couldn't seem to resist.

In fact, as he sat there, looking into her eyes, trying to find the answers to all the questions in his mind, all he could think about was that he wanted to kiss her again. To lower his head, to pull her closer, to never let her go.

"Why?" He wasn't supposed to care. That wasn't a question he was supposed to ask. He was just supposed to take whatever she gave, be happy with it. But he didn't want whatever she gave, it wasn't enough. He wanted more. He wanted everything.

"Why what?" she asked, a little confused judging by the dip of her brows and the pursing of her lips.

How could she even wonder what he was asking why for? Why did she kiss him? Why had she rejected him earlier if she wanted to kiss now? She wasn't the kind of girl who went around kissing random men. At least, she hadn't used to be that kind of girl.

And even as he thought back, he knew she hadn't changed that much. Yes, she was different from when she was in high school. More mature, more vulnerable, more determined to accept life the way it came and to thank God for everything He gave her. He'd found that out about her, and it had only made him love her more.

He couldn't think of words to answer her question. How was he supposed to say, why did you kiss me? Why did you reject me earlier? Those questions made him too vulnerable, and he'd already been hurt enough.

Just as quickly as the rain had started, it was over, and he could even see a splash of sunlight trying to creep in under the kayak.

"It's over," he said, shifting to his knees, having to lean closer to her before he could lean away, lifting the kayak with his shoulder, and grabbing a hold of both sides so he could flip it. It landed bottom down on the ground.

"Trevor," she said, her word a question, a demand, but he ignored it. He just didn't think he could take any more. Although, all of him wanted to try.

"Our parents are waiting for us in the truck. Depending on how wet they got, they're going to want to go home so they can change out of their wet clothes. It won't be good for your mother to be sitting around wet."

They could turn the truck on and turn the heater on and be just fine, but he didn't want to sit here with her any longer. Yeah, he wanted to run away. To get away from her. To protect himself and his tender, delicate feelings. The ones that had been trampled by her back in high school and again now.

Why couldn't he love someone who would love him back?

Twenty-Two

Saturday morning, Grace was helping her mom set the table for brunch, but she was still thinking about the kayak trip and how she messed everything up. Why couldn't she say how she really felt? Why was she so afraid?

She figured she knew. After all, a person didn't go through the kind of pain that she'd gone through with her husband cheating and leaving her without having some kind of scars and issues to show from it. And she assumed that's how it was manifesting itself, by pushing Trevor away, because she automatically assumed that he was going to hurt her. But in their relationship, it had always been the other way around, and on Friday, she had, true to form, hurt him again.

He didn't want to talk to her, didn't want to hear it, and she was only hoping that she would be able to talk to him today, when he came with his dad, and find some way to tell him how she really felt.

Maybe it was too late. He certainly hadn't acted like he was interested in hearing anything from her. Although, he'd allowed her to kiss him.

She wanted to touch her fingers to her lips, but her mom was coming in with a fruit salad to set on the table, and Grace was supposed to have the plates and silverware arranged for her sisters and Don and Trevor who were going to show up anytime.

"I think we have everything." Her mother looked over the table, her eyes shining. She was excited, because she was going to be telling her daughters about her boyfriend.

Grace had thought that maybe it would be a good idea to tell her daughters first and then invite them to a meal, but her mom had insisted that the meal was the best idea.

It would be a fine idea, as long as both her sisters were okay with her mom's relationship. If either one of them had any doubts or reservations, it was going to get awkward. But her mom couldn't see that. All she could see through her love-tinted glasses was the fact that she was in love and she wanted everyone to be happy for her.

Grace said a small prayer that Stacy and Jill would be kind, even if they didn't agree. She didn't want to see the excitement and happiness torn from her mother's face.

There was a perfunctory knock at the door, and then it opened. Jill and Stacy walked in together.

"Did you guys drive together?" Grace asked as she walked over to greet her sisters.

"No, we just have the same timing apparently," Stacy said, using her free arm to hug her sister. Grace was surprised, but she hugged her back. "I brought some Danishes, because I couldn't show up with nothing." She held up the box in her other hand.

"I bet if you take those to the kitchen, Mom can find fancy plates to put them on." Grace spoke as she leaned toward Jill and embraced her as well.

"That's where we differ, because I didn't bring anything. I just got off a twelve-hour shift at five o'clock. I grabbed a couple of hours of sleep before I got up to come here."

"Doesn't sound like enough sleep," Grace said, looking at her sister with concern. She hadn't considered that as a nurse, she probably didn't work regular hours the way everyone else did.

"I'll be okay. I just can't stay very long, because I need to go back and sleep some more. I'm going in again at five o'clock this evening."

"That's a rough schedule," Grace said, walking toward the table beside her sister. She really did want to have a better relationship with her sisters. She'd reached out to her friends, but either the phone numbers she had were old and not any good, or they didn't answer. Since she hadn't spoken to either Claire or Lauren.

But her sisters were right in front of her, and she intended to do her best to start building something that would last. The reason they didn't have a relationship was her fault. Her and her arrogance, running out of town thinking she was better than everyone else.

"But it's very rewarding work. Although, it's stressful."

"That's not good for your health," Grace said, thinking of the irony of someone working as a nurse and the work itself making them less healthy, more likely to need a nurse.

"I know. I love the work right now, but I do have an eye out for a nice, cushy office job with a good doctor. Something like that would be less stressful than working in a hospital. I can handle it now, but I can see that as I get older, I'm going to want something else."

"It's good that you're able to see that," Grace said, wishing that she was somehow capable of seeing what was good for her and what she needed. Unfortunately, she consistently made bad choices. And really had no idea of what she actually wanted or what was best for her.

She could see all of those mistakes scattered throughout her life. She wanted to ask her sister how she got so wise and how she figured things out. But her mother came over, embracing her sister.

"What's this big news you have?" Stacy asked, coming out from the kitchen where she'd gone to set her Danishes down.

"You'll find out in just a few minutes. I wanted to come out and greet Jill and chat a bit before...well, before," her mom said, her eyes shining.

"Do you have any idea what this is about?" Stacy asked Grace point-blank.

Grace fidgeted. She knew exactly what this was about. But she could feel Stacy's displeasure, and she didn't want to get yelled at.

"Don't you worry about it. Everything's going to come out in just a few minutes. Now, come to the kitchen with me while I find a plate to arrange your Danishes on and tell me what's going on in your life. Because pretty soon, it's going to be all about me."

Her mother put one arm around Stacy and one arm around Jill and guided them into the kitchen. Grace trailed along behind, not feeling left out. After all, she would have her mother to herself all week, and her sisters had to go back to their actual lives.

Maybe there was an advantage to being at rock bottom and having nowhere else to go. She didn't have anything to take her away from her mother, as she did when she was younger. It felt like a reward to get to be with her.

Stacy and Jill chatted about their lives as their mom found a plate and arranged the Danishes artistically on it. Her mom had a flair for that, and Grace had inherited it. Jill and Stacy would probably just serve them from the box.

Not that there was anything wrong with that, because there wasn't. It was just something that Grace had that made her feel like she was a little gifted. And made her feel a little less jealous of her sisters' successes in life. Sure, she screwed up. She made some bad decisions and had things go in a totally wrong direction. But that didn't mean that she couldn't change things and turn them around.

And that included talking to Trevor and seeing if she could work things out. No. Admitting that she had feelings for him. Strong feelings, and that she wanted to have a real relationship, not a fake one. And not just friends.

She smiled a bit as she thought about their kiss under the kayak. It wasn't exactly romantic, with the wet and the wind and the crunched-up way they were sitting, but in her mind, it was absolutely perfect. It couldn't have been better. Unless he would have wrapped his arms around her and kissed her like he meant it. Instead of just allowing her to kiss him.

"You must be thinking of something really nice with that sappy smile on your face," Stacy observed, and Grace realized that she was smiling for no reason, since she was not paying the slightest bit of attention to what everyone was saying.

She didn't have to answer though, because there was a knock at the door. This one was not perfunctory, and all the ladies in the room turned to look at it.

"I'll go answer it," her mom said before anyone else could say anything.

"What is going on?" Stacy asked, drilling her eyes into Grace's. Growing up, Stacy was a bit of a taskmaster, a control freak, the boss, the way the oldest child typically was. Grace had been trained to listen to her, and the look that she gave her now was intimidating, reaching back into her childhood.

But somehow, she found the presence of mind to smile and shake her head. "This is Mom's surprise. Just relax."

Her sister did not like that at all, mostly because she didn't like not being in control, and she definitely didn't like Grace knowing something that she didn't, which Grace could see clearly from the look she gave Grace before she turned toward the door.

She gasped softly. "That's a man," she said, to no one in particular, although she said it under her breath as Don walked in.

"Don!" their mother exclaimed, and she threw her arms around him like she hadn't seen him for six weeks instead of less than a day.

"Gita Baby," Don said in that slightly sexy, slightly sultry tone that Grace was actually getting used to. Maybe it didn't sound so bad after all. She wouldn't mind someone talking to her in that kind of voice. No. She didn't want just anyone talking to her in that tone of voice. She wanted to hear it from Trevor, and for her and her only.

"What's going on?" Jill asked as Don and Gita embraced.

"Girls, I wanted you to meet my boyfriend, Don Gillett."

"We know Don. We grew up with Trevor and his siblings," Stacy said, moving forward. Maybe she realized that what she had said wasn't the most polite thing, because her tone modulated as she said, "But it's good to see you again after all these years." She put her hand out, and Don shook it. Then, as though what their mother had said finally penetrated, she said, "Did you say your boyfriend?"

"Mom has a boyfriend?" Jill didn't seem to be able to believe it either, but her words were softer and probably didn't carry across the room. "That's...crazy wild."

"I know," Grace said, thinking about how long it took her to get used to the idea. She didn't figure her sisters would jump into it any quicker, but no matter how many times she told her mom that she thought that her mom should tell them privately before she sprang her boyfriend on them, her mom insisted that they would be happy and excited for her.

"I guess if you're happy, that makes me happy too," Stacy said, seeming to take a moment before she wrapped her arms around her mother. "I really am happy. You look like you're glowing."

"I'm in love. Isn't that what people in love do? Glow?"

"I guess. But it's an odd look to see on my mom," Stacy said, obviously trying to be kind but having a little bit of a hard time.

Grace bumped Jill. "You'll get used to it. Don really is a good guy."

"I'm just so shocked," Jill said as she seemed to force her feet to move slowly across the floor. "Mr. Gillett. It's a pleasure."

"You can call me Don. I expect that we're going to be family very soon."

Jill's eyes got huge, and Grace wished he could shove those words back in his mouth. They were just getting used to the idea that their mother had a boyfriend, and she knew how shocking it was for her to see her mom with someone other than their dad. The idea that the man was going to take her dad's place was probably a little more than what they could handle right now.

"Oh. Okay," Jill said, obviously struggling for words.

"Don has been so good to Mom. This is the happiest I've seen her in years," Grace said, coming over and hoping that her sisters did not point out that she barely ever visited her mom or saw her, so she wouldn't know whether she had been happy all the years that she had been gone or not.

Thankfully her sisters seemed to be so discombobulated by the fact that their mom had a boyfriend, or by seeing their mom hugging and glowing like a teenager in love with someone other than their dad, that they didn't point out the obvious untruth beneath her words.

"It makes me happy to know that someone's making Mom happy. She deserves it. She's the best woman I know," Jill said, her words still reserved, and she nodded at Don, as though she were warning him.

She did hold her hand out, and Don shook it, putting his free hand over top of hers and leaning close as he said, "I know what a treasure she is. And trust me, I have no intention of taking that for granted."

Grace wanted to say that Don's wife had left him after thirty years of marriage, and that he knew heartbreak, and that she thought that one of the lessons he had learned through that was that there were things that he could do to make his marriage better. But she didn't know whether it was the time or place, and also at that very moment, she realized that...Don was alone.

Trevor hadn't come.

She actually stepped away from the group and looked outside just to be sure he wasn't still hanging out by the door or something. She pulled the door closed when she realized it was true.

He wasn't there.

Immediately she realized that she probably shouldn't have expected him to come. After all, why would he have? They had confessed to their parents that the relationship was a farce, designed only to get their parents together, and now that was out in the open, there was no need for them to pretend anymore.

She had wanted Trevor to be there. She had expected to be able to talk to him, had been counting on it. Disappointment, deep and hard and hot, swirled in her chest and filled up her stomach with a tar-like substance that made her insides cling together.

Now what? When was she going to be able to see him to be able to tell him how she felt and to ask him to give her a chance?

Maybe she shouldn't. Maybe his absence was answer enough. That he had enough of her and was done, done with her and the pain and hurt that she'd inflicted on him over the years. Although, she didn't know that he even felt anything for her. After all, she kissed him, and he'd let her, but he hadn't really kissed her back.

She had been telling herself that she just surprised him and hadn't allowed herself to think that maybe he hadn't wanted to. Maybe he'd been too polite to pull back and tell her that he didn't want to kiss her, but by his lack of interest, he'd shown her that he was over her and didn't want to go back down that road.

Regardless, she had to push that out of her mind, because this was her mother's day. Her mother was glowing and happy, and she wanted her daughters to be happy and excited for her, and Grace was going to do her very best to not let her mother down.

Twenty–Three

"How did it go, Dad?" Trevor asked, his eyes on the coatrack he was making, although he did glance at his dad as he walked into the shop. There was no mistaking the smile on his dad's face. He didn't need to hear his dad say it went well in order for him to know that it went well, very well.

"I think they liked me," his dad said.

Trevor couldn't shake the feeling that came over him for just a couple of seconds at the idea of his dad trying to impress someone else's children rather than his own. At the idea of his dad being in someone else's family, with their kids being his stepchildren.

It felt…wrong. He had never before stopped to consider how it might affect a person whose parents were working on making a different family than the one that they were used to.

How hard it must be for children whose parents got divorced, and then they tried to put a different family together. No wonder divorce was hard on children.

"Of course they liked you, Dad. Everyone likes you." He couldn't think of a single person who didn't like his dad.

"There's a first time for everything, and when I have so much riding on it, when I care so much, you can't help but be nervous, you know?"

"Yeah. I know what you mean." Sometimes the things that meant so much to them were the very things that God didn't give to them. He didn't really understand, other than to think that maybe God just wanted to test them and make sure that they weren't putting anything ahead of Him.

"I'm glad."

He wanted to ask if anyone asked about him, but he just kept working on the coatrack in front of him. Making sure he got the details right, giving it more concentration than what it actually required.

"So are there wedding bells in your future?" he finally asked. And he wasn't jealous. He really did want his dad to be happy. After what his mother had done, he felt his dad deserved all the happiness in the world. Of course, his mother had burned her bridges, since she had very little or no relationship with any of her children.

"I wish you would have gone. You would have been welcome."

"Did anyone ask about me?" He didn't want to ask that question, but he made up for that by trying to put as much disinterest as he could into his voice. All of a sudden, the coatrack got exceptionally more interesting.

"No. I guess they didn't."

"That's what I thought." He sighed.

"I wish there was something I could do. Grace is such a nice girl, and I really feel like you guys would be perfect together."

"I thought that too, but apparently the lady doesn't feel the same, so I just need to accept that. Unless I fight it, and that's kind of silly, since you can't make people feel things for you that they don't feel, you know?"

"It's a hard lesson to learn." He paused, coming over to the workbench and watching over Trevor's shoulder as he worked. Normally he didn't care for people looking over his shoulder, but he actually welcomed his dad. His dad was not the kind of person who was going to criticize him, but he would give him helpful tips if he saw anything that could be improved.

"Some people never learn that lesson," his dad continued, his voice thoughtful. "It was what I had to learn when your mother left. She didn't give me much warning, any, if I remember correctly. I felt like I would have been blindsided anyway. And I did beg her to come back. Begged her to not break up our family, begged her to reconsider. I prayed and prayed, and I was sure that God would answer my prayer, because after all, I was asking for something good. I was asking for my marriage to be reconciled, for my family to be put back together, something that God wanted, which is a marriage and family intact. He hates divorce. So why would He allow mine?"

"There's a good question. I think you had a point. But… God didn't put your marriage back together." He had never thought about it that way before, but his dad was right. Why wouldn't God answer that prayer? It was obviously God's will for any marriage to stay together.

"I can't answer that. All I can do is say that I have to continue to have faith that whatever God allows has to be the right thing. Even if it feels like something that's very wrong." His dad shifted, coming around more beside him and leaning against the workbench, folding his arms over his chest. "I learned a lot through that time in my life. I think a lot of times when we go through pain, those are some of the most intense learning times that we have."

"Too bad we can't learn without pain," Trevor said, not wanting to acknowledge how bad his own heartbreak felt. His chest had been on fire since the moment Grace had said that they weren't anything and sounded like she meant it with her whole heart and soul.

"I think without pain, lessons don't stick. He makes us desperate. I read once where one of those royal Russian families were being invaded by the enemy. The father, the king, knowing he was probably going to be killed, was hiding something important and wanted his daughter to remember where it was. He knew that she probably wasn't going to remember unless it was associated with something terrible, so he took his own knife and slashed across her hand. And then, once he had done that, he looked her in the eye and told her where he was hiding the treasure. He knew that was the only way he could make sure that she remembered where it was if it took years for her to get back to the throne."

"Wow. That's pretty brutal." He didn't know whether he could slash anyone's hand, let alone his own, innocent daughter's, and especially if that was going to be her last memory of him before he was killed.

"That's what a loving father does. He doesn't think about himself, and sometimes you can't think about the immediate comfort of your children. Because if that daughter was ever going to grow up and resume her rightful place on the throne, she was going to need to know where those royal doodads that he was hiding were. Without them, she couldn't claim her right to the throne. He was doing her a favor, it just didn't seem like that way at the time."

That made sense. As much as he didn't want to admit that the pain of losing Grace again, or since he couldn't really lose what he didn't have, of not getting Grace, was for the best.

He had to believe that. That God was allowing him to feel the temporary pain so that God could do something greater later on. It was sad comfort but something that he would be wise to remember in his life. God was in control of everything, and when things didn't go his way, it didn't mean that God hated him, or that he should get upset or angry, but that he should just have faith and trust the Lord to work all things out for his good.

"I'm sorry, son," his dad said, putting a hand on his shoulder, as though he knew exactly what Trevor was thinking.

"Dad, I'm happy for you. I don't want you to be sad right now. This is an exciting time for you. Your new family loves you, and you've got a girlfriend that you're hoping to marry soon."

"I did want to talk to you about that," his dad said, dropping his hand and moving away a little, looking at the shelf where the sandpaper and sanders and various nails and screws were stored.

"About what?" Trevor asked, wondering if he had missed something.

"I was thinking about asking Gita to marry me."

"Don't you think it's kind of fast?" Trevor asked, trying to figure out exactly how long Don and Gita had been seeing each other. For real, not for fake.

"Maybe it feels fast to you, but it feels like forever to me, and I'm not getting any younger. Plus, it's not like Gita is someone I just met and I don't know anything about her. I know she's a solid, upstanding, God-fearing woman, who is living for Jesus. That's what I want. Hopefully she knows the same things about me and feels just as comfortable with me as I do with her."

That's all a person really needed. To know that someone loved Jesus, and to know their history was even better.

"When you put it that way, it makes sense."

"And I guess at my age, I can't help but think that every day that I don't spend with her is a day that we're wasting, because I don't have an unlimited number of days. No one does. It's just that when you get to be this age, you really realize that for real."

Trevor hadn't gotten to that age yet. The years of missing Grace, and wishing that she was his, seemed to stretch out endlessly in front of him. He didn't exactly wish that his life was shorter, but a shorter life would mean less pain.

"I guess I'm not old enough to understand that yet," he said, and he couldn't help that his voice sounded a little depressed.

"The right girl is going to come along, one who appreciates you and loves you for who you are. Sees what you are and thinks you're the greatest ever. I don't know why Grace can't see that, but it seems like she's always looking beyond you for things that are better. It makes me mad, even though I love her and think she's a wonderful person."

"Thanks." That was the right answer, but he didn't much feel like thanking his dad. Because he really wanted to hear his dad say, *I think Grace actually likes you. She's just doing a good job of pretending she doesn't*. Or even better, he could say, *Grace admitted to me that she really does like you. And regrets the things she said.*

Of course, there was that kiss. What was with that?

It almost felt like a goodbye kiss to him. He hadn't wanted to participate in anything like that. It would have been like loading the gun for the firing squad to shoot him. Well, maybe not that terrible, but still, it felt like an ending rather than a beginning, and he didn't want endings with Grace. He wanted beginnings. For the rest of their lives.

"That looks nice," his dad said, indicating the coatrack that Trevor held loosely in his hands now.

"There's just something I was thinking about. I wish I had more artistic talent, to paint some flowers or something right here where the header is. It would look a lot better."

"Grace has that talent," his dad said and then shook his head. "I'm sorry. I just always thought the two of you fit so well together. I'll try not to say things like that in the future."

"Dad. It's okay. I'm not some little snowflake that's going to crumble if you mention something that I don't want you to. Talk about her if you need to. And if you're getting married to her mom, you're going to be seeing her a lot, I would assume, since I think she's moving in with her mom permanently."

"That's what her mom said, and Gita seemed to be pretty happy about it. Of course, I'm not sure what's going to happen since Gita and I plan to live together, and you live with me and Grace lives with her... That could get a little crowded at the breakfast table."

Trevor didn't miss the glint of humor in his dad's comment. He tried to laugh along with it. "Whichever house you guys choose to live in, I suppose Grace will stay in her house, and I'll stay here, so you only have one of us."

"The other one's going to visit."

"Yeah. I suppose they will." He didn't want to think about how awkward that would be. Maybe he had jumped the gun and shouldn't have planned to move back to spend so much time with his dad.

"I can see you're thinking right now that maybe you should see if you can get your job back and move back to the 'burbs, but don't even think that way. I want you here. Need you."

He didn't know how much his dad actually needed him, but he did know that if his dad said he needed him, there was no way Trevor could say no.

"I'm not. I love it here, and I love being here with you. And these are supposed to be the years you and I spend together."

"I hope you don't mind if Gita is involved in those too."

"That'll make me happy." It wouldn't make him happy if he had to see Grace, especially seeing Grace with some other man.

He needed to stop thinking about that though. He needed to figure out a positive way to spin it. Wasn't that what Grace was telling him? That she figured out how to see things in a positive manner and focus on that? That's what he needed to do. That, and to let her go, and just accept whatever God allowed in his life. Because God always did what was best.

"Some things just are meant to be," Don said, clamping a hand on Trevor's shoulder and squeezing, before he walked out of the woodshed.

Twenty–Four

"I hope you don't mind, but it's been a huge day, and I think I am going to head upstairs and go to bed," Gita said.

Grace and Stacy still sat in the living room. Grace stayed, mostly to be polite and not go to bed before their "guest." Not that Stacy was a guest. Still, she didn't know why Stacy was staying so long, but she didn't want to be rude.

But now that her mother was heading to bed, surely Stacy would head out too. After all, she had at least an hour drive to get home.

"It was so good to see you today, Mom. And I'm thrilled about Don. Sorry it took me a little bit to get my equilibrium back. It's...weird to see you with someone that's not Dad. But it's thrilling to see you so happy." She stood up and went over and gave her mom a hug.

Even though Grace lived there and saw her mom every day, she stood up and went over to hug her mother as well. She supposed one of the things that she had learned was that a person never knew when the last time was the last time. She didn't want to not show love to her mother just because she assumed there would be another day.

Why couldn't she have applied that to Trevor? She should have said everything that she needed to say while they were under the kayak. Better yet, she should have said it before she left the picnic area. She should have admitted that she was scared, that she was afraid and uncertain, and not made it sound like she didn't want to have anything to do with him, ever. She wished she hadn't been terrible. No wonder Trevor hadn't come today.

Their mother left, and Stacy turned to Grace. "I wanted to talk to you a little bit privately."

"Oh. Okay," she said. She could just imagine that Stacy had all kinds of criticisms and suggestions and things that Grace had not been doing correctly. In fact, if Stacy knew that she'd allowed her mother to get in a kayak, Stacy was probably going to flip her brisket.

"Do you mind if we sit down for a little bit? I know it's late, and I don't want to keep you up but... You don't have a job to go to in the morning."

Just a week ago, she might have thought that her sister was saying that to be mean. But she could hear the tenderness in her voice, and a little bit of uncertainty, like she didn't want to rub in anything that was hurtful. She appreciated the consideration.

"Of course you can sit down. You can stay as long as you like. What did you want to tell me?" she asked as she seated herself on the couch while Stacy perched on a chair.

"First of all, I wanted to tell you what a great job you've been doing with Mom. She is not in any pain, and she said her physical therapist was surprised and impressed at how well she was doing. I knew that Mom was determined to do as well as she could, but it seemed like progress had been slow while I was here. But she's just seemed to flourish under your care."

Grace knew she was supposed to say something, but she was having trouble wrapping her mind around the fact that Stacy had just given her a compliment. And not just a run-of-the-mill, casual compliment, but a really big, huge, nice compliment.

"Thanks. I...read a book that talked about how important it was for seniors to be active, and so whatever the physical therapist cleared her to do, we've been trying to make sure that she did, not that I am trying to exhaust her every day, but... She just loves being out, and this is a good time of year. It probably wouldn't have been successful if it were winter."

"Winters here can be brutal, that's for sure," Stacy said, shivering as though the memories were that close, and they were. Really.

"I agree," Grace said, wondering if that's all Stacy wanted to talk about.

She had tried to reach out to her friends, and they didn't answer, but her sisters were right in front of her. She had tried to keep that in mind all day as they interacted. So the Lord hadn't opened the doors for her to reach out to Lauren and Claire, but Stacy and Jill had been right in front of her. She didn't think God could make it any more clear that he wanted her to start with her family.

That thought made her focus on Stacy even more. She saw that Stacy's fingers were twisting, and it seemed like Stacy might have been a little bit nervous.

"Is everything okay?" she asked.

"It's fine."

Stacy was there without her husband. Although she had said that her kids had soccer games and her husband was going to the games while Stacy came to see her family. There really wasn't anything weird about that, unless there was.

"I guess I wanted to ask how Trevor was. I know it's not my business," she said, moving her hands so that they were open and flat. Like she didn't have any ulterior motives. "I just always thought that the two of you were so good together, and every time I thought about you, I was sad it didn't work out. I always got the impression that he would take you back at any time, not to lay the blame on you. I just wondered if you'd reconnected with him since you've been back."

Grace didn't say anything for a moment, mostly because she wasn't sure what to say. After all, she had connected with Trevor, and she'd managed to screw it up a second time.

Then she remembered what she had been thinking about her sisters. She wanted to have a close relationship with them, and here was Stacy, reaching out, trying to help, or at least caring about her enough to ask.

Why couldn't she tell her what her issue was?

She briefly explained that she and Trevor had met and then decided that they would try to pretend to be together so that they could trick their parents into spending more time together, which had been successful apparently, but she ended with what she had done after they were kayaking, although she did not mention the kiss. That felt...too private.

"Well, as you can see, I'm back to my old tricks. Doing stupid stuff that drives him away."

"Then stop it, and go after him. You know he wants you."

"That's just it. I really don't."

"Did he give any sign at all that he didn't?"

"He didn't try to talk me into it once I said what I did while we were kayaking."

"Do you want a man who can't take no for an answer? You said a clear no, he respected your boundaries. If you put boundaries down that you didn't want to have down, it's your job to go tell him that you are wrong, that you want him, that you love him." Stacy paused. "If you do. I'm not suggesting you lie."

"I know. Do you really think that that's what I need to do? I always thought the man should chase the woman."

"Women do like to be pursued. To know that their man really wants them. But you told him no so many times. You don't want him to disrespect your no, right?"

"I kind of do." But she understood what Stacy was saying. When she said no, she wanted that to be respected. At the same time, she wanted him to chase her, which didn't make sense.

"Sometimes I don't understand myself."

"I think women are so complicated they can't even get themselves figured out. Because we want to be able to say no and yet have the man know when we actually mean yes, but sometimes we say no and we mean no, and we want them to know that too." Stacy smiled, like she hadn't just said something really complicated.

"You're going to be a really great mom of teenagers."

"Good thing, since I'm going to have a teenager next year."

"Where did the time go?" Grace asked, wondering how her life had gone by so quickly and she missed it. Or not missed it, just...wasted it. Wasted time on her ex when she should have been spending that time on someone who appreciated her. On Trevor.

"I can't answer that, but I can say you don't want the rest of your life to fly by while you make wrong decision after wrong decision." Stacy scrunched her face up. "No offense. I assume that you agree with me that walking away from Trevor the first time was a wrong decision."

"Yeah. I can see that now easily." Grace was surprised at how easy it was to admit that. Maybe that showed the maturity she gained, because when she left, she wouldn't have admitted that she was doing anything wrong, and for years afterward, she felt the same. Admitting she had been wrong showed weakness. She didn't want anyone to see any weakness in her. So, she would insist that she was right no matter how wrong she was. Talk about dumb.

"I think I've matured some. Maybe I give myself too much credit." She smiled in a self-depreciating way. After all, she thought she knew everything when she left. Now, anytime she felt like she had arrived at all, it made her feel like maybe she was just as wrong as she was before.

"I think it's hard to know when we're deceiving ourselves and when we've truly learned. But I do think that you want to do your best to try to make things right with Trevor. Especially if you feel for him the way I think you do."

"I always have. I don't know why I felt like success outside of Raspberry Ridge was more important than the people here. I'm sorry. That included you, and I wasn't very nice for a while."

"It's fine. I know I've messed up plenty of times in my life as well, and I don't see you lording it over my head at all." She laughed. "You could tell me how bossy and controlling I was when we were growing up and how bossy and controlling I still am. My family doesn't hesitate to tell me."

"In a loving way, I'm sure. There are times where we need bossy and controlling people in our lives, and there are definitely times where I appreciate your bossy controllingness." She paused. "Maybe now, when I really needed someone to tell me that I was being ridiculous by expecting Trevor to know that I said no but I meant yes."

"I wouldn't hesitate to go tell him that I was wrong. Of course..." Stacy sighed.

"He might not feel the same way anymore."

"I suppose. Or he might not want to take another chance on you. I don't think his feelings would have changed that much in this short amount of time, but... I guess that's a chance we have to take when we miss our opportunities."

"True."

Stacy stood to her feet and stretched. "I better get home. My family is going to wonder where I am. And I'm going to need some of my bossy controllingness to get the house put back in shape, because it never is cleaned to my standards when I'm gone."

"Or maybe you could just lower your standards and love your family," Grace said with a bit of a gleam in her eye.

"That's good advice, little sister," Stacy said as they embraced, and they chatted for a bit more before Stacy left.

Grace went to bed feeling lighter than she had for a while. She had a plan anyway. She needed to talk to Trevor and lay everything out on the line. She needed to be vulnerable and humble, which was not going to be easy. And maybe even apologize for her arrogance and pride. Not just for her arrogance and pride of her teenage years, but of the last few days. And then, it would be up to Trevor as to what happened.

Twenty-Five

Trevor glanced at his phone where it sat on the workbench, a message from Grace lighting up the screen.

His entire chest lit up as well. He tried to calm himself down. After all, she might be going to tell him that she never wanted to see him again, or that they were going to need to figure out how to navigate the waters of their parents having a relationship and her not wanting to see him, or she might be wanting to tell him that she wanted their parents to move into his house, so she would never have to see him.

Why did all the negative things have to go through his head? Why did he focus on those things?

He set the tool he'd been using down and picked up his phone.

He sent the message back, trying not to think about it too much. He'd just focus on what he was doing and let things happen the way

God wanted them to. God knew what he wanted, he prayed for it enough, but he needed to accept God's will, if that's what it was.

Would today work? Eleven o'clock?

Trevor glanced at his phone when it dinged and then glanced at the time. An hour from now.

He wished she would have said now, so he didn't have to sit and think about it for sixty minutes.

He grabbed his phone and typed a quick message.

I'll be there.

He sat back down and tried to focus on the stool he'd been making. Furniture seemed to be more his style, since the crafty things he could do, but he couldn't decorate. His dad was right, he and Grace would make a great pair, since he could make the bones, and she could make them look beautiful.

Still, making furniture was nice as well. And he loved working with wood, taking pieces that didn't look like anything, and seeing the potential inside of them. He liked thinking about how they used to be trees, growing in the woods, reaching out to the sky, maybe home for squirrels or rest for a bird or a place for deer to rub their antlers on. Now, they had a second life in the home of a human family, bringing joy and beauty to wherever they ended up.

The whole life cycle fascinated him, and he was honored and happy to be a part of it.

The next forty-five minutes crawled by. He almost quit ten minutes early, but then what in the world was he going to do? It would only take ten minutes to walk to the healing garden, and if he left too soon, he would be early. But five minutes early was better than fifteen minutes early, since he would get there and start pacing, upsetting anyone who had been going there to find peace and quiet and comfort. He didn't want to do that. The healing garden meant too much to too many people for him to despoil the serenity folks found there.

It was an interesting choice for Grace to make, and maybe in a way that showed how much she wanted to get along and not fight when she said whatever it was she had to say.

Maybe she had something good to say. Something he wanted to hear. He tried to tell himself that, although he had a hard time convincing himself that that was true. But maybe he just needed to let go of his expectations and show up. Just show up with no preconceived notions and no thoughts on what he expected from her.

Or on what he expected from himself. Other than to be kind and compassionate, no matter what.

He found himself walking faster than he normally did down the street toward the healing garden. Even if he got there early, he could enjoy the beauty and serenity, and it could help calm his soul and prepare him for whatever Grace wanted.

But to his surprise when he arrived, she was already there. There were no cars in the parking lot, so when he walked around the turn and saw a woman standing with her hands behind her back, looking at the waterfall, his favorite spot, he knew it was Grace even before she moved, and the sunlight caught her hair, shining like a halo around her head.

His heart skipped a beat. It probably always would every time he laid eyes on her. He didn't think he'd ever be able to get it to stop.

Maybe he should move somewhere far, far away. But he wouldn't do that until after his father was gone. Because he wasn't going to leave his dad. That was the reason he moved back. He wasn't going to be a coward and run from a woman.

"Trevor," Grace said as she turned, her hands going to her throat, her eyes opening wide. "You're early."

She almost looked like she wasn't expecting him. He had said he was going to be there, hadn't he?

"So are you," he said, stating the obvious.

"I know. I was hoping to draw a little inspiration and maybe calmness and courage."

Courage? What did she need courage for?

He walked over, stopping within five feet of her. Plenty of space between them, but not so much that they couldn't hear each other over the sound of the water. It was soothing and beautiful and absolutely perfect. Vera and Dominic had done an excellent job in designing it.

"Maybe that's what I was thinking," he finally said as he turned toward the water, putting his hands behind his back. He didn't know what else to do with them, because he was tempted to touch her. And that wouldn't be appropriate.

"Thank you for coming. I appreciate it. Especially after what I said at the picnic."

"You were just saying what you meant. How you felt. There's nothing wrong with that. No one expects you to pretend something you don't feel."

"That's just it. It was a lie. It was a lie just like the lie I told when I left town when I was a teenager in high school. I went flying out, all arrogance and confidence, but in reality, I still loved you. I wanted to stay. I just somehow thought that success in the world was more important than finding a man of integrity and character." She smiled and laughed a dry, humorous laugh. "Obviously my life has taught me lessons that I wish I would have known then. Lessons like character and integrity are far more important than material success. That finding a man with those qualities is harder than you think. And when you find someone like that, when you're in love with someone like that, and they're in love with you, you should hold on as hard as you can."

Her eyes lifted, and they met his, and he felt that connection the whole way to his core.

"When I came back, I felt it again. I thought that maybe you were feeling the same way, and then... I decided that you weren't. I don't know. I guess I'm confused and don't trust myself and what I see and feel, because I've been so wrong in my life. But one thing I know for sure, if you're willing to take a chance on me, I love you, and I'd like to be with you. However you think that should look."

She stood before him, meeting his eyes for one more second before she lowered her head, her own hands clasped behind her back, her posture slightly stooped as though she were standing in humility before him.

He didn't like that posture any more than he liked the arrogant thumbing her nose posture, but he understood what she was saying with her words and posture. That the next move was his, and she would be humble and submissive to whatever it was. He supposed that left a lot of room for him to manipulate or be unkind, but it also showed that she trusted him, and it showed her humility and sorrow for what she had done.

He didn't know what to say. Or where to start. This was basically his dream come true, but... It almost seemed too good to be true.

"You love me?" he finally said, supposing that was the most important thing. After so long of wishing and wanting and waiting, she was finally saying that she loved him? Or had he misheard her and not fully understood that what she was saying was not only did she love him, but she loved him when she left, and she regretted it?

That changed everything.

"Yes. I love you. I'm so sorry for the stupid way I've acted. Stupid when I was younger, stupid just the other day. Just stupid all around. I wish I could guarantee that I wasn't going to be stupid ever again, but I'm afraid I probably can't. My history speaks for itself."

For the first time, there was a bit of humor in her eyes. One of the things he loved about her was that she wasn't afraid to laugh. That she laughed easily at herself, with a self-deprecating humor that he found endearing.

"That's one of the things I love about you. Maybe I don't want you to change it." He wasn't sure whether that was true. He didn't love that she had left for so long, but he did love that she was apologizing and admitted that she loved him when she left. That soothed his heart and soul in a way that nothing else ever could.

"I suppose you can see that in me for the rest of my life." Now there was no denying the twinkle in her eyes.

"I hope I can. I hope this means that you're going to spend the rest of your life with me." That was jumping the gun. They were just getting together, and here he was demanding that she devote her life to him.

But she didn't seem put off by the idea.

"That's what I love about you. One of the many things. You know what you want, and it's not a flash in the pan and then it's gone. You're not jumping from woman to woman to woman. It's just me."

"It's always been you."

He thought about how when she had left it was like the sun had set in his life, had gone below the far horizon, and now, it was like it was still below the far horizon, but on the eastern side, and he was just waiting for the sun to come up and for them to start their life together. The same idea, but totally different feelings.

"I know. You've never wavered. While I've waffled back and forth and up and down. All over." She lifted her shoulder and looked down.

"I don't care. I have enough steadfastness for both of us."

"We don't need it. Because I'm set on you, for the rest of my life. However long that is."

"Hopefully a really long time," he said, grinning a bit, because he had every intention of living for decades longer and expected her to as well. He took a step forward, touching her arm. She twisted her hand and moved so that their fingers linked together, tightening a bit until he took another step toward her.

"You're bossy," he said.

"Oh, you haven't seen anything yet," she said, and he had to laugh. She really wasn't bossy or demanding or controlling. Maybe she had been a little success oriented and defined success in a way that he didn't, but she wasn't the kind of person who tried to make others do what she wanted.

"I just wanted to remind you that I'm divorced, with no job, no money, and a terrible credit rating."

"Is there anything else you need to tell me before I kiss you?" he asked, not caring about any of that. They could work through anything. Work through whatever they had to in order for them to be together. The important things were already taken care of. She loved Jesus, so did he. God would be the center of their life. Everything else they could figure out.

"No," she said softly.

"Good," he murmured, tugging her toward him before letting go of her hands and wrapping his arms around her, burying one hand in her hair as he lowered his head and kissed her. It wasn't a question kiss, and it definitely did not feel like a goodbye kiss. It felt like a hello to the rest of his life kiss, although it made his hands shake and his knees tremble and he had to end it way sooner than he wanted to just so he could remain upright.

He leaned his forehead on hers and waited for a bit until he caught his breath again. "I don't think we should kiss like that in public. It's kind of dangerous."

"I agree with you completely," she said, and he was gratified to hear that she sounded like she was out of breath as well.

"Still, today is a bit of a special day, and maybe another kiss might be in order."

She laughed. "He changed his mind already? I thought he was steadfast and had enough of that quality for both of us."

He smiled. She was teasing him, and it warmed him to the very tips of his toes.

"Shut up and kiss me," he whispered before he kissed her again.

Twenty-Six

Grace could not keep the smile off her face. It had been three days since she and Trevor had met in the healing garden, and they'd spent a lot of time kissing.

Those memories were sweet, and she thought about how the healing garden really had healed so much of their relationship. Of course, she had to hand it to Trevor, he had forgiven her easily and completely without requiring her to jump through any hoops or make any specific promises. He'd just taken her at her word and trusted her.

She wasn't sure whether she would have been able to do that or not, but she appreciated the fact that he had, and she promised herself that she was not going to let him down. Ever.

They had decided that because their parents' relationship was so new, they would wait a few days before they announced to their parents at least that they were together.

It had been an extremely long three days, but she and her mother were going to Trevor and Don's house, and they were making supper for them. And they were going to announce their relationship status at the meal.

Beyond that, she would need to tell her sisters, and he could tell his siblings, and they would move on from there. They didn't have a timeline, other than they didn't want to wait forever. They'd already wasted a lot of time apart from each other. Both of them agreed that they wanted to be done wasting time.

"This cauliflower seems to be a tradition at the meals we have with Don and Trevor," her mom said as she opened the door and held it open while Grace walked through after a perfunctory knock.

"I kinda like it. Not just the fact that it's tradition, but the cauliflower itself. So good. I think I could eat it pretty much every day."

"I like it, but I don't know if I like it that much," her mother said, walking beside her without limping at all. Her hip was almost as good as new.

"Gita Baby!" Don said, coming around the corner and putting his arms up and embracing her mother in a huge hug, which her mother did not hesitate to return.

Every time Grace saw them together, she had to smile and be so happy for her mom. After all, after the heartache and sadness she had with losing their dad, it was so nice to see her happy again and with a man who deserved her.

"Donnie. It's so good to see you." They looked into each other's eyes as Trevor came around the corner, looking absolutely adorable in a black apron with pictures of grilling tools on the front.

Grace supposed she would think he would look dashing in anything, but the apron really made him attractive.

"Grace," Trevor said, and she realized that she needed to talk to him about getting her a cute nickname the way her mom had. After all, nothing said I love you more than a nickname that only the two of them shared.

Although, the way he said her name made her fingers tingle, and maybe she didn't need a nickname after all.

"Trevor. Hello," she said, feeling suddenly self-conscious, which was ridiculous. This was Trevor, who always made her feel so at ease and to whom she could say anything.

She felt awkward standing there and wanted to go and wrap her arms around him, but her parents didn't know about them yet, and they had agreed that they would tell them this evening, not show them.

"You ladies need to come in. Supper is ready. Perfect timing," Don said as he put an arm around Gita and walked into the dining room with her beside him.

Trevor and Grace followed behind, exchanging looks and smiles and all the secret things that people who are in love do.

Grace didn't think that this would ever be her again, and she vowed once more to be careful to nurture her relationship, and not take advantage of it, and cherish it the way she knew she needed to. Not everybody got a second chance like this.

They sat down, Don said grace, and they started to eat.

Grace had only taken a mouthful when Trevor said, "Grace and I have something to tell you two."

"That's funny, because Gita Baby and I have something to tell you two," Don said, putting his hand over top of Gita's hand which was beside her plate.

"All right. Did you want to tell us now?" Trevor said, glancing at Grace with his brows raised. They weren't expecting this. They were expecting that they had given their parents enough time to get used to their relationship before they stole the spotlight with their own.

"I think we can, Donnie," Gita said, smiling.

"All right then. I'll just say it. I asked Gita Baby to marry me last night, and she said yes."

"Wow," Grace said, putting her hands together and trying to pretend it was a clap and not out of shock. She was not expecting that, but her mom had said something about life getting shorter and not wanting to waste any days, and she felt the same way about her own relationship. Plus, there was no doubt that Gita and Don were perfect for each other.

She smiled sincerely. "Congratulations! I'm so happy for you."

"Thanks," Gita said, beaming at her daughter and then looking back at Don.

"That's awesome, Dad. I am surprised it's so soon, but it feels like perfect timing." Trevor sounded like he was telling the truth, and Grace believed him. After all, she'd never heard him lie. Unlike her ex. That was just one difference, a major one, but one of many.

"Thanks. We figured you two would be happy for us. Now we have to announce it to the rest of the family. I didn't want to wait, so I'll probably call your sisters this afternoon."

"And I'll call your siblings as well. We're probably going to have a wedding within a week or two, since we didn't want to drag it out. But we wanted everyone to know before we actually got hitched."

"That's considerate of you," Trevor said.

"Anyway. That's our news. What's yours?" Gita said as she and Don continued to hold hands.

Was it okay to share the news of their own relationship? Grace only hesitated a moment before she felt certain her mother would not mind in the slightest and would actually want to know. "I said some things to Trevor on our kayaking trip that weren't true. And I got enough courage to talk to Trevor about them."

Trevor smiled at her, and she kinda stumbled. She hoped he would take over, and he seemed to read that on her face.

"We decided that we are going to be together. I haven't asked her to marry me yet, Dad. You're faster than I am, but I suppose that'll be coming, because that's the direction our relationship is headed. That's our goal, right, Grace?"

He lifted his brows, as though wanting to make sure that he wasn't saying anything that she didn't agree with. She appreciated the fact that he was careful and concerned about her.

"That's right. Although, I'm a little bit upset that you allowed your dad to beat you."

"Maybe I want to get a ring first. I noticed that your mother doesn't have one."

"I told him not to worry about it. At my age, jewelry doesn't mean anything at all. I have plenty of rings but no husband. I'd rather have a husband than a thousand rings." Her mother gave another sweet smile to Don.

"You're getting a husband, and you'll have a ring if you want one. I just didn't want to force you to wear something you didn't want."

"It never even occurred to me that you might not want a ring." Trevor looked at Grace.

She lifted her shoulder. "A ring says to the rest of the world that you're married, but I guess having a ring for a ring's sake doesn't really mean anything to me. It's just for what it says to everyone else."

"A wedding ring, then, but not an engagement ring?"

Maybe they should have this conversation in private, but she wasn't going to shut him down. And she didn't care if Mom, and now her future stepfather, heard.

"Yes. That would work just fine. Honestly, I don't care. Having the husband, like my mom said, is the most important thing. A husband with character and integrity, someone I can depend on, someone who will be honest with me and keep his word. I would take that over a thousand rings any day, too."

"Sounds to me like we're in agreement," her mother said, looking over at Grace.

Grace looked around the table, at the family that had been cobbled together. She thought about how hopeless her life had been not that long ago and how hopeful it looked now. It was funny how just a few turns of the earth happened and everything was different.

Maybe it wasn't so funny after all, since God promised to work everything together for her good. Sometimes she just had trouble remembering that.

Twenty-Seven

"I now pronounce you man and wife. You may kiss the bride."

Don's head lowered and she lifted hers, and they shared a chaste but warm and happy kiss as the living room erupted in claps and cheers.

There weren't a whole lot of extra people at the wedding, just Grace's sisters and their husbands and Stacy's children, along with Trevor's siblings and their spouses and children as well. Don had one sibling who had come in for the wedding, and Gita had a couple siblings there with their spouses as well. All in all, it was less than thirty people. But that made the living room very crowded.

"They look good together, don't they?" Trevor leaned down and whispered in Grace's ear. He loved having her beside him and had been watching her more than he'd been watching the couple in the front say their vows. She had been deeply interested and engaged, and had almost seemed on the verge of tears a couple of times.

The wedding didn't move him nearly that much, but it made him want to have a wedding of his own.

"They do look good together. And they look so happy."

"Have you changed your mind on a wedding ring?" he asked, wondering if he maybe should get her one anyway. It seemed like sometimes women said things that they didn't really mean, and they wanted men to figure out what they actually meant, which was ridiculous, since they often said the exact opposite of what they meant.

"I was serious. I just want you."

"Would you marry me?" he asked, his voice low and his inner critic telling him that he couldn't have picked a worse time.

But Grace looked up at him with shining eyes and was nodding her head even before the word passed her lips. "Yes."

He smiled. She hadn't said that he had picked the wrong time or that he hadn't been very romantic or complained about anything like that. She just seemed happy that he had asked and that they would be getting married. In his opinion, those were the things that they should be happy about. The trappings, the ring, the perfect setting, all that, was just...distraction. Or show. And maybe, maybe Grace had enough of that.

"Can we set a date soon?" she asked, lifting her head as her breath whispered along his neck, making him draw her closer to him.

"Yeah. Let's do that."

She leaned back, and they shared a look that said that they would be talking about that the next time they had an opportunity.

That had to be good enough for him.

"Have you ever seen Mom look so beautiful?" Stacy came over and stood in front of them, glancing back at the couple at the front of the room, who were accepting congratulations from the people around them.

"She's practically glowing," Grace said as Trevor casually listened. Stacy was nice, and her husband was okay, and he would get along with them because they were Grace's family, but he would stay out of the sisters' conversation unless invited in. He didn't have that much experience with women, and sometimes their conversations, rather than going in a straight line, took the route of a gravel mountain road, with switchbacks and lane changes and U-turns and lots of other things that would lose a man who wasn't used to such things.

"And by the way, I'm happy to see the two of you together. Finally," Stacy said.

Jill came over and heard Stacy's last comment. "It's about time. The two of you are perfect together, and I can't believe it's taken you all this time to figure it out."

"I'm a little slow, but I hope to make up for that by getting your sister to marry me sooner rather than later."

"Good luck with that. And by the way, you guys should join forces and make crafts together. It's been obvious to everyone that Mom needs someone to take over her craft business, and Grace is the perfect choice, but you would take everything up a notch and allow Grace to offer things that Mom never could."

"We haven't talked about that, but we'll have to, won't we, darling?" he said, unwilling to take his arm out from around her waist, no matter how many people were crowded into the room or how warm it got. She didn't seem like she minded, since she pressed against him.

"I think that's good. I couldn't imagine anything better than getting to work with you every day."

"That's what I was thinking." They hadn't talked about where they would live, but it seemed to make sense that whatever house their parents moved into, they would buy and live in the other one. He really didn't care, as long as Grace was by his side.

Neither one of them mentioned that he had just asked Grace to marry him. He supposed Grace felt the same way he did, not wanting to take attention away from their parents' happy day. There would be plenty of time for them to make their announcement some other time.

"Attention, everyone. Can you listen for a second?" Gita stood in front of everyone. The room quieted down as people stopped to listen to what she had to say.

"Don and I are so honored that you came here to share our special day. We have food available in the dining room. It's a buffet-type meal, where you just grab your plate from the stack and pick what you want. Be sure to get some of the crockpot pepper jack cauliflower, since it's our signature relationship dish. It...has grown along with us." She smiled at Don.

"And Gita made it herself, so be sure to compliment the chef, although don't compliment her too much, because I don't want to take her spotlight away from me."

Laughter rippled throughout the crowd as Gita gave him a look that said that no one could outshine him in her eyes.

"I hope we're that cute when we're old," Grace said, looking up at Trevor.

He hadn't exactly been thinking that same thing, but his words were true. "I hope so too." And somehow they reminded him of something he had wanted to tell Grace earlier. "Oh. I know what I wanted to tell you. I heard that Claire was back in town. Did you hear that?"

"No. I didn't," Grace said, sounding shocked.

"It's just a rumor that's going around. I haven't actually seen her. And I haven't made it out to her grandmother's house to check. I did think that you might be interested, since I overheard you mentioning something to your mom about you trying to get in contact with her and Lauren and not being able to get a hold of either one."

"Thanks. I appreciate you hearing that and remembering. I'll definitely try to see if I can make it out to go visit her. Maybe I have an old number that's been disconnected or something."

Trevor leaned down to Grace's ear. "Are you sure you're okay with that? I know that you love your friends, but there are some memories involved there."

She seemed to appreciate his caring concern. He didn't want her to get lost in all of the sadness and tragedy that circled around when the three of them got together. Even though they'd been friends long after the tragedy had occurred, it seemed to get bigger over the years. Sitting like a mountain between them.

He knew he thought about it more than once, even though he hadn't been directly involved. He also knew that even in high school, it had bothered Grace, and she talked to him about it more than once.

"I can't believe that you remember the things I said to you way back when."

"That would be something that would be hard for anyone to get over. But yeah. I definitely remember. You always got sad around the time of the anniversary. And you didn't enjoy going on the water like you did before."

"It was attached to a lot of bad memories. But I did have a good time kayaking with you and our parents. I'd really like to do that again."

"Maybe we can get married on water?" Maybe that was a bad idea, but surely if they made a point of attaching good memories to the water, it would overcome the bad memories.

"As long as there's no storm. Although there was a storm while we were kayaking, I really enjoyed it. Although...you didn't kiss me back?" She looked up at him, as though finally asking why.

He didn't have a problem answering her. He remembered exactly why. "It felt like you were saying goodbye. I didn't want to participate in that. I didn't want to admit that it could have been the end."

"Why did you think it was goodbye?"

"You had just said that we weren't a couple, didn't have a relationship, and when we got in the kayak, you didn't want to talk about it. So that was where I thought you were. And... I guess I just thought that you were sealing it with a kiss, as crazy as that sounds." Looking back, he realized that that probably was a ridiculous idea on his part. But it was the truth. It was exactly how he felt.

"I'm sorry. I can see how you would feel that way, but no. It was... me not being able to resist you, I guess."

"I like the idea that you find me irresistible. I kind of feel like we ought to find a spot where you can show me exactly how irresistible I am."

Despite the happy celebration of the day, he was tired of all the people hanging around. He wanted to have Grace by himself. So he could kiss her whenever he wanted to and hold her in his arms without making the people around him uncomfortable.

"I think that's a really good idea, but I think our parents would be a little bit upset if we disappeared on their wedding day. We probably ought to at least make a bit of an effort to mingle."

He could see in her eyes that she was still thinking about Claire too. He figured, once they got out of here, she'd want to go see her friend.

"All right. You're right, as usual. Still," he said, then he leaned down and put his lips on her temple. He couldn't resist, but that would have to do until later when there were not quite as many people around.

Hopefully, they would have a lifetime of laters.

THANKS SO MUCH FOR READING! If you would love to stay in Raspberry Ridge just a little longer, and if you'd like to see what happens with Claire - does she get a second chance at love? - you can order Over the Verdant Hills HERE.

A Gift from Jessie

View this code through your smart phone camera to be taken to a page where you can download a FREE ebook when you sign up to get updates from Jessie Gussman! Find out why people say, "Jessie's is the only newsletter I open and read" and "You make my day brighter. Love, love, love reading your newsletters. I don't know where you find time to write books. You are so busy living life. A true blessing." and "I know from now on that I can't be drinking my morning coffee while reading your newsletter – I laughed so hard I sprayed it out all over the table!"

Claim your free book from Jessie!